STORM'S TARGET

AMELIA STORM SERIES: BOOK ELEVEN

MARY STONE

AMY WILSON

Copyright © 2023 by Mary Stone Publishing

All rights reserved.

No part of this book may be reproduced in any form or by any electronic or mechanical means, including information storage and retrieval systems, without written permission from the author, except for the use of brief quotations in a book review.

❋ Created with Vellum

To all nature enthusiasts...may this story add excitement to your adventures without diminishing your love for the wild. Here's to the enduring beauty and mystery of the great outdoors.

DESCRIPTION

Hunting season is open, and humans are the game.

In her new role with the Bureau's Violent Crime Unit, Special Agent Amelia Storm is ready to focus on new types of crimes—ones that aren't mob related. She didn't, however, expect her first case to take her to rural Illinois, where the tranquil waters of Lake Henry have been guarding a grim secret.

Three corpses...and that's just the beginning.

Among the deceased are two recent victims, a young couple last seen camping in the nearby wilderness preserve. A third, a grim echo from years past, is a set of bones picked clean and left to whisper secrets of an older, darker crime. The only connection between the victims, besides the location of their bodies, is the ancient rune carved into their skull. Shockingly, a ViCAP search of the distinctive symbol reveals eighteen sets of linked murders occurring over the past decade.

All murdered in pairs.

As Amelia and her partner delve deeper into the case, a disturbing realization dawns—they aren't hunting a lone serial killer but two. Working in tandem, these predators stalk their victims under the veil of darkness.

Now the interval between murders is shortening, and the killers are escalating. Amelia must turn the hunter into the hunted...before they target their next victims.

From the wickedly dark minds of Mary Stone and Amy Wilson comes Storm's Target, book eleven of the Amelia Storm Series. But be forewarned. You may never go camping again.

1

The chilling bite of the night air prickled Jeremy Fitzgerald's skin, turning every drop of sweat into a cold shard. His heart thundered in his chest, a reminder that he was still alive...for now.

Out of breath and nearly out of hope, he forced his legs to forge deeper into the impenetrable maze of the forest. But was he delving farther into safety or into danger? The darkness gave no answers.

Slivers of moonlight shined through the canopy of leaves and branches overhead, casting ghostly silhouettes that seemed to reach out, threatening to grasp him, while offering little light to illuminate his path. The ground beneath was treacherous, every step a gamble—he could be seconds away from plummeting into an unseen abyss.

Then he'd never find Leslie.

She'd been beside him when they'd begun their race away from the campsite clearing. But now? The void had consumed her too.

Panic tightened its grip, strangling every thought as he searched for her. The disorientation intensified. Was he retracing his steps, or was he stumbling deeper into the predator's lair? Despair stung his eyes, but he blinked away the tears. He had to find Leslie. Every moment lost was a moment closer to whatever terror had pursued them seizing its prize.

Leslie...

Whispers of the wind seemed to echo her name.

Where are you?

Jeremy's lungs burned as he dragged in a much-needed breath. Every muscle in his body was on fire, even the parts he was certain he hadn't used in the desperate escape from his and Leslie's camp. Christ, how long had he been running?

As he raised his left foot to take another step, his toes slammed into the exposed root of a tree.

Pain jolted up his leg, sharp as a bolt of lightning. He flailed, teetering on the edge of a face-first plunge into the dirt. His palm scraped against bark, and he grasped the trunk of the tree that had tripped him, using it to haul himself back to his feet.

Wheezing, Jeremy held onto the tree as if clutching a life preserver in the middle of the ocean.

This was pointless. His entire desperate journey away from the campsite meant nothing if Leslie got hurt. He didn't have any semblance of a plan.

How had this happened?

He remembered hearing something rustling outside their tent. Remembered grabbing his phone and cursing when the zipper of the tent got stuck.

Leslie had palmed her pocketknife, joking that she'd have to cut them out.

And she had.

The sudden slice of a blade tearing through the side of

their tent had sent panic surging through them both. Leslie —always clever—used the pocketknife to slash through the damn door panel. They'd run away side by side, until...

Jeremy gritted his teeth. He was scared shitless. And though his instincts screamed to keep running until he collapsed or found help, he couldn't rely on his caveman brain to get him or Leslie through this night alive. He needed to catch his breath, and more importantly, he needed a plan. Something more concrete than *run until you can't.*

Leaning against the rough bark of the tree, he scanned the woodland.

He and Leslie weren't the most outdoors-savvy couple on the planet, but they enjoyed hiking, fishing, and camping when their busy schedules allowed. They were also aware of a few fundamentals of wilderness survival—chief among them being to always maintain a sense of direction. A compass was a basic tool, but it could make the difference between surviving or dying.

To Jeremy's chagrin, he hadn't thought to reach for his compass when a machete-wielding maniac attacked him and his fiancée in the middle of the damn night. He'd only grabbed his cell.

Hope bloomed in his chest.

With a trembling hand, Jeremy patted the pockets of his sweatpants.

"Holy shit." The words were barely a whisper, his voice cracked and small. As his hand closed around the smartphone, he permitted himself the first glimpse of optimism so far that night.

Though Lake Henrietta—a body of water not far from the Mississippi River and a popular destination for hikers, fishers, and campers alike—felt remote, Jeremy and Leslie's phones had both received a strong signal when they'd set up their tent earlier.

As Jeremy fumbled with the device, he clenched his free hand into a fist. The entire traumatic situation had left him trembling, his pulse drumming in his ears like the bass line to a heavy metal song. Though adrenaline had fueled his escape from the lunatic with the machete, fine motor movements like entering in a PIN to unlock his phone were challenging.

On the fourth try, the dial pad gave way to the home screen of Jeremy's cell.

The four bars of service he'd noted earlier in the day were gone, replaced by the *no-service* icon.

Fuck!

An overwhelming sense of hopelessness tightened his throat. There was no way he'd run far enough to put himself out of his carrier's service area, was there?

Jeremy stuffed the phone back into his pocket. Without service, it was useless. And with no clue as to his whereabouts, so was the compass.

Raking a hand through his sweat dampened hair, Jeremy pushed away from the tree. Though he didn't know where he was headed, he had to keep moving. The longer he stayed in one place, the more likely he was to be found by the man chasing him. And it had definitely been a man. As they'd fled, Jeremy had caught sight of a hulking figure built like an NFL linebacker as he destroyed their new four-person tent.

Rather than resume his chaotic pace, Jeremy moved through the darkness at a swift walk. He strained his senses for any signs of Leslie or, God forbid, their attacker. Other than the soft crackle of grass beneath his feet and the chatter of night birds, the woods were quiet.

Were they too quiet, or had he simply missed the relative calm while he'd been running for his life?

Without the thunder of his pulse deafening him, Jeremy became acutely aware of how loud his movements were. No matter his effort to tread carefully, something gave him away with each step. A twig, a dried leaf, the swish of his pajama pants, even the squelch of mud. Maybe he was better off sprinting.

But what would happen if he ran headlong into a low-hanging tree branch and knocked himself unconscious? Hell, he'd damn near done that only moments ago. Now that he'd eluded the madman from camp, he was better off not risking his welfare for a little extra distance.

A light crackle from off to the right snapped him to attention. Anxiety and adrenaline froze his tired body in place as he strained to make out the source of the disturbance. Thin overhead leaves, just starting to grow for summer, allowed more of the moon's glow to reach the ground. Still, the meager light wasn't enough to make out any distinct shapes.

He stood as still as a corpse, only his eyes flicking back and forth. As the agonizing seconds dragged on, nothing stirred. Not an animal, not a murderous psychopath with a long silver blade, not Jeremy's lost fiancée.

Just...nothing.

Flexing his hands, Jeremy swallowed against the oppressive dryness in his mouth. There was a distinct possibility a raccoon or a deer had made the noise, but with the experience from camp so clearly etched in his mind, he wasn't keen on dismissing it.

He needed to keep moving.

After a few more steps, he caught another faint sound. A new sound.

Running water. Muted at first but clearer as Jeremy trudged onward. When he conjured up a mental image of the map of Lake Henrietta and the surrounding area, he recalled a smaller river near the lake, the Grove River. There were a handful of creeks in the area, as well, but the rush of water was too strong to belong to a small creek. Even if it did, Jeremy didn't care. One of the rules of survival he'd learned was to follow rivers and creeks when lost.

If memory served, Grove River fed into the Mississippi in one direction and wound its way from a small town in the other. In either case, he was confident he could find his way to civilization if he followed the river.

With cautious optimism lending him renewed energy, Jeremy hurried toward the running water. Trees loomed tall on either side of him, but directly ahead, the moon's glow illuminated a grassy clearing.

Jeremy had every intention of double-checking his surroundings to ensure the madman and his machete weren't lying in wait just out of sight before approaching the river's bank. Though the clearing seemed like a reprieve from the confusing tangle of woodland he'd navigated so far, open space would also make him an obvious target to any crazy backwoods murderer who might've been hot on his trail.

Slowly, painstakingly, he neared the clearing. As he emerged from behind a tall oak, his view of the grassy area was unobstructed.

His gaze snapped to the form of a body crumpled a mere six feet from the line of trees.

Breath caught in his throat, Jeremy could only gawk at the still form.

Is it a deer?

Don't be stupid. It's human.

Maybe Leslie overpowered the guy with the machete?

Of their own volition, his feet took him toward the body. With each agonizing step, his mind screamed for him to turn and run, that whatever was in front of him, he didn't want to see. That he couldn't deal with this reality. Not right now. Not with a psychopath still on the loose.

Reality clarified as he drew close—the body was too small to belong to the madman.

After fully emerging from the woods, now just a dozen feet away, Jeremy realized with a sickening sense of dread that the still form was that of a woman. As a wispy cloud drifted past the moon, the glow shined on the body's light hair.

Jeremy had found Leslie.

A million thoughts whipped through his head at Mach 3, but he could only focus on checking if Leslie was still alive. Her form lay still, but in the low light, Jeremy could easily overlook the slight rise and fall of her chest. And though she was out in the open, patchy shadows obscured her.

Jeremy sprinted out from his flimsy cover behind a pine tree.

Halfway to Leslie, a man's voice stopped him.

"Ah, what exactly do you think you're doing, kid?" The tone was laden with mocking derision. As the man's tall form came into view, Jeremy knew why. Though he hadn't caught much of the machete man's face, this person's black hoodie, cargo pants, and combat boots were exactly the same as what he'd spotted outside the tent.

Jeremy's head swiveled back and forth from Leslie to Machete Man.

Moonlight caught the red-tinged silver of the wicked

hunting knife as Machete Man held his arms out wide, a sickening smile on his face. "What? Nothing to say?"

Far too late, the pieces clicked together in Jeremy's head. The red stain on the knife, the dark shadow by Leslie. Not a shadow. A pool of blood.

As if without a care in the world, Machete Man strolled toward her. "You know, I'm a little disappointed in you, Jeremy. When I saw you and your girl set up camp earlier, I thought for sure you'd put up a good fight. But look at you. Standing here with your thumb up your ass."

His words fanned the fires of rage that burned in Jeremy's stomach. He wished he could charge at the smug son of a bitch and throw him headfirst into the river. Hold him under the surface until he gasped for air...then do it again.

But the man had a good six inches on him, not to mention the discrepancy in muscle mass. He was built like a brick shithouse. And the clean-shaven face—he probably wasn't some backwoods hillbilly. Oh, plus the giant knife.

Jeremy knew a losing battle when he saw one. He had a single hope.

Run. Make it to a town and tell the cops everything.

Whipping around, he ran. But he stopped cold when another shadow emerged from the woods he was heading back into. The new figure was clad in all black, just like Machete Man, but notably smaller.

She raised a weapon—Jeremy could swear it was a crossbow—and took aim at him.

Jeremy skirted to the side and lost his footing on the soft earth, but the movement paid off. The air beside his face whistled as a projectile flew past his head and over his shoulder.

"Shit!" He regained his balance and hurtled toward the trees.

The woman in black muttered something Jeremy couldn't make out, and for a beat, he thought he might actually make it to the woods.

Except, a couple of feet from the relative cover of a few old pines, something slammed into his shoulder with enough force to spin him nearly one hundred and eighty degrees, dropping him to his knees. Fire blossomed from the site of the collision.

Fighting the excruciating pain, Jeremy scrambled up and turned back toward the woods.

He made it one step before another rush of searing fire slammed into his ribs. Falling to one knee, he wailed as he grasped desperately at his side. Blood crept up the back of his throat like bile, and when he tried to drag in a breath of precious oxygen, he was greeted with a wet sucking sensation in his chest. The pain from his shoulder and his ribs coalesced into one white-hot inferno that threatened to incinerate his consciousness.

Jeremy blinked...or at least, he intended to blink.

When he opened his eyes, he was no longer kneeling in front of the line of trees. Instead, he was face to face with his fiancée's glassy, lifeless stare.

How had he gotten here? He'd been trying to get away from where Machete Man was lording over her body.

"You're still in there, aren't you, kid?" Machete Man chuckled, a low rumble in his throat. "Well, you won't be for long, so let's get this party started, shall we?"

"Hurry up." It was the woman, sharp and impatient.

Jeremy didn't hear what she said after that. His limbs had grown cold, his teeth chattering from a chill he'd never before experienced.

When Machete Man took hold of Leslie's hair, waving the blade in Jeremy's face, Jeremy noted for the first time a gaping wound beneath his fiancée's chin. In the dimming moonlight, it looked like darkness itself trying to claw its way out of her neck.

Jeremy wanted to say he was sorry, that they should've gone to her parents' lake house instead of on a stupid camping trip. His dumb idea. But as he opened his mouth, only a wet gurgle came forth.

As his grasp on reality slipped away, he could've sworn Machete Man slid his blade across Leslie's forehead. He struggled to hold his heavy lids open as a dark liquid oozed from the cut like sludge, blanketing the love of his life's face until all went black.

2

Resting both hands on her hips, Special Agent Amelia Storm peered down at the travel suitcase flung open at the foot of her bed. Her go bag was beside it, but it sure wasn't "go" ready.

"Someone needs to kick my ass."

In all fairness, she'd been pretty busy the past few weeks. She'd had big case after big case, and the mountains of paperwork that followed had taken up almost every moment of the last ten days. But still...

She checked her watch and cursed. She had less than half an hour to get back to the Bureau. With Chicago's traffic, she'd probably still be late even if she left this very instant.

"Which is why you must have your go bags ready for any contingency." Lord, how many times had her Quantico trainer preached that to her?

No matter how often she'd traveled during her time with the FBI—not to mention the ten years she'd spent in the military before that—she was always worried she'd forget an essential item. Her toothbrush, deodorant, socks, even shoes.

Anytime she traveled, she always triple- and quadruple-checked her suitcase to ensure she wouldn't have to make an *inconvenient* trip to a convenience store.

Forgetting socks or shampoo wasn't the end of the world, but Amelia figured everyone had their little irrational worries when traveling. Besides, her diligence over the years was likely the reason she hadn't wound up leaving an essential item behind.

Until today.

When she'd walked into the FBI office that morning for her first day as a full-fledged member of the Bureau's Violent Crime Unit, she hadn't expected to have to travel for her newest case. The Chicago field office served Cook County as well as the northern portion of the state of Illinois, but usually there was more than enough work in the city to keep her and her fellow agents occupied. Cramming millions of people into a relatively small space had that effect.

Standing in her bedroom, Amelia returned her focus to the suitcase. "Let's see…shampoo, conditioner, toothbrush, toothpaste, deodorant…" She tapped each item as she listed it, shuffling through the excessive amount of clothing she'd packed to ensure she'd put together proper outfits.

"Good lord, how long are you going to be gone? A month?" The familiar voice pulled her attention to the bedroom doorway. Though Zane Palmer had worked at the Chicago Field Office for as long as Amelia, hints of his native Jersey accent still tinged his words.

Amelia groaned as Zane shot her one of his trademark grins. Even though she was glad to see him before she left, she didn't want him to witness her last-minute scramble.

Leaning against the doorframe, he loosened his royal blue tie. He looked handsome in his tailored Tom Ford suit. Only now, the smooth black fabric was decorated with cat fur.

On cue, Amelia's long-haired calico, Hup, slipped into the room, no doubt leaving another patch of fur where she brushed along Zane's leg. Chances were, Zane would spend a few minutes with a lint roller before returning to the office.

Amelia let out a huff of feigned exasperation. "What are you doing here?"

With a look that made her insides go twisty, he strode up to her. "I couldn't let you leave without a goodbye kiss."

She gave him a playful shove that didn't move him an inch. "I've got no time for kissing or anything else. Can't you see I'm panic packing?"

He glanced at the bed. "I can see that. Where's your go—"

"Don't say it." She poked him in the chest. "And please don't tell my Quantico instructor that I've failed FBI 101 so badly."

He pulled her closer. "If you don't let me kiss you, I'm definitely telling."

Rising onto her tiptoes, she pressed her lips to his. "There. Satisfied?"

"Never." But he let her go.

"Besides, I'll probably be gone a few days, so I'll need more than the go bag holds. What if I spill coffee on one shirt when I only packed two?" She shot him a knowing look, and his grin only widened. "I'd rather have way more clothes than I need than be stuck trying to wash a shirt in a hotel room bathroom sink."

Amusement glittered in his gray eyes as he held up his hands in surrender. "Okay, okay. Fair enough. How about you take your time, and I'll drive you back to the office? That'll save you some time finding a parking space."

Her shoulders relaxed a little. "That would be fantastic."

A ball of orange, white, and black fur in the corner of Amelia's vision drew her attention back to the suitcase as Hup crept toward the neat pile of clothes.

Zane winked. "I think she wants to go with you."

"No," Amelia moved toward the cat, preparing to scoop her up before she could snuggle into the suitcase, "she just wants a new bed. Because the four other cat beds and the couch aren't good enough for her."

Hup narrowed her eyes at Amelia's hands but let her owner pick her up. With a cross between a meow and a squawk, the cat hopped down to the floor and trotted out of the room.

"Wow, you just got rejected." Zane glanced over his shoulder at the departing feline. "Don't worry, I'm sure she'll be meowing for you twenty minutes after you're gone."

A twinge of guilt prodded Amelia at the thought of abandoning her cat. "According to the briefing this morning, the sheriff's department in Jordan County is still searching the lake where they found two bodies."

Amelia's phone pinged. Zane lifted an eyebrow. "Want me to get it?"

"Please."

As she pulled another pair of socks from her drawer, Zane whistled. "They found another body."

"Please tell me you're kidding." When he simply handed her the phone, she read through the entire message before tossing it on the bed and continuing to pack. "Okay...*three* so far, and they're still looking. They've got divers from the state police helping with the search. One of the locals was out fishing last night, and that's how he found the first victim."

"A fisher?" Zane's eyebrows scrunched together. "How'd he find a corpse?"

Amelia had posed the exact same question when Dean had given her a rundown of the situation that morning. "He and his kid were out on a boat, and one of their lines got snagged on something. According to his statement, he tugged on it, and it seemed to come free. A few minutes later, a corpse floated up beside their boat."

Leaning against the doorway, Zane brushed some cat fur from his leg. "Wow. That's an unpleasant surprise. I bet that's a fishing trip they won't forget anytime soon."

"No kidding. Jordan County will be sending the bodies to the Cook County M.E.'s office, since they don't have the staffing and resources we do."

Zane rubbed his chin, appearing thoughtful. "How long have the bodies been in the lake?"

"Well, the M.E. estimated the first vic had only been dead for a couple days. We probably won't get a more precise time frame."

Like the flip of a switch, Amelia's brain shifted from civilian mode to federal investigator as she recalled the grisly details she and her case partner, Special Agent Dean Steelman, had gone through that morning.

Fortunately, Zane was on the same wavelength, and the mental adjustment was as natural for him as it was for her. "What about the second body?"

A photo of the gray-green, waterlogged corpse flashed in Amelia's mind. "It was pretty badly decomposed. The coroner figured she'd been there for a couple weeks, at least."

As Zane wrinkled his nose, Amelia suppressed a laugh.

Even though the subject matter was bleak, he always had a way of keeping her even-keeled and grounded. The murders in Jordan County were the first major case she'd been assigned to work without him since they'd investigated the kidnapping of Leila Jackson nearly a year ago. Though Amelia was excited for this fresh chapter in her life, the new focus of her work would undoubtedly take some adjustment.

She was especially grateful to be getting away from mob cases. Having cleared the air with Alex Passarelli—a Capo in the D'Amato crime family and her ex-boyfriend from high school—she figured the time was perfect to pivot to new types of crime.

Pushing aside all thoughts of Alex, she nodded toward her phone. "According to the message, the third victim we just learned about has been dead for about the same amount of time as the first Jane Doe. About two days."

Zane let out a low whistle. "Three bodies in a lake in rural Illinois? What the hell's going on out there?"

"The place is called Lake Henrietta. It's a wilderness preserve next to the Mississippi River. There's the lake, a few hiking trails, a good-sized patch of woodland, even a smaller river. All kinds of activities for outdoor enthusiasts." Amelia raised her shoulders in a dramatic shrug. "And apparently some psychopath decided it was a good spot to dump their victims' bodies."

"Apparently." Zane met her gaze, shaking his finger like he was a scientist who'd just uncovered one of the world's great mysteries. "And *that* is why we can't have nice things. We get a nice place out by the Mississippi, and what happens? Some serial killer ruins it by dumping bodies in the lake."

Even as Amelia laughed at his theatrics, she had to

admit he had a point. "Well, that's why Steelman and I are heading out there. It's a small department, so they don't have specialists who've worked on cases like this before. We're going to help out the sheriff's department as much as we can and hopefully get a lead on whoever's responsible for the murders."

Though a slight smile remained, Zane's expression sobered. "Does it look like they were killed by the same perp? Or are we thinking Lake Henrietta has become a popular dumping spot for multiple killers?"

"It's the same killer." Amelia's amusement evaporated as she recalled the photos from the body retrieval.

Zane lifted an eyebrow. "How do you know?"

"The victims were scalped and have the same symbol carved in their skulls."

Zane groaned. "A symbol? Carved in their skulls? Any idea what tool they used? A screwdriver? A chisel?"

"We're not sure yet. We probably won't have an idea what was used to carve the symbol until the forensic anthropologist gets a closer look. That's why Dr. Islas from the Cook County medical examiner's office is headed out there to assist the local coroner."

Though Zane made no secret of his disdain for serial killers, Amelia had to admit part of her found them fascinating. Her entire tenure in the FBI had been spent in Organized Crime, where she'd dealt with one powerful crime syndicate after another.

In Chicago alone, the mob's influence ran so deep it was virtually impossible to extricate its tentacles from the foundation of the city itself. Amelia and Zane had dealt the world of organized crime a hefty blow when they'd taken down a handful of powerful mob allies, but how long would that last? How long would it take before another sick bastard took Brian Kolthoff's spot as a corrupt D.C. billionaire lobbyist whose only loyalty belonged to himself and his bank account?

Zane was good at dealing with the mafiosos. No matter how hopeless the situation appeared, he didn't hesitate to jump right back in the ring to duke it out all over again.

As for Amelia? She'd grown tired of playing the same game of Whac-A-Mole. She was proud of the work she'd done, and she was damn pleased with the fact that she'd helped rid the world of corrupt senator Stan Young and his lackey, dirty FBI agent—*former* agent—Joseph Larson.

It would take the criminal organizations in the city awhile to regain their lost influence, and for the time being, Zane and the rest of the Organized Crime Division would be there to meet them head-on.

But Amelia was done beating her head against that brick wall. Her involvement with the Italian Mafia had started when she was fifteen years old, when she'd met the son of a D'Amato family capo while working at a movie theater. Her relationship with Alex had shaped the rest of her life, and finally, at age thirty, she could say with confidence that she was a stronger person for the experience.

Shaking off the thoughts, Amelia zipped her suitcase closed and turned back to Zane. "All right, I think I've got everything. Steelman said he wanted to leave by one, and it's," she glanced at the digital clock on one of the two nightstands, "twenty until twelve."

With a lazy salute, Zane stepped aside to let her through the doorway. "Let's get you back to the office so you and Steelman can go catch this lunatic."

3

At one o'clock on the dot, Amelia and Dean set off from the Chicago FBI Field Office. According to the GPS, the trip to Henrietta City—which wasn't a city but a town of approximately three thousand people, according to Amelia's internet search—was slated to take around three and a half hours.

Since her transfer to Chicago the year before, Amelia had become accustomed to using her time in the passenger seat to conduct case research. Whether she was running background checks on a victim's friends and family, reviewing the rap sheet of a potential suspect, or even making phone calls to check on alibis, she preferred to use Chicago's atrocious traffic to her benefit.

Unfortunately, Jordan County officials hadn't identified the three corpses they'd pulled from Lake Henrietta yet. The details surrounding the murders were slim, and as such, Amelia's ability to research was hampered significantly. Sure, she could look up details about the Lake Henrietta Wilderness Preserve, but multiple descriptions of the Illinois state bird didn't move the investigation forward.

As Dean merged onto the interstate, he blew out a long sigh. "Are you a road trip kinda person, Storm?"

Amelia studied the cars and trucks zipping along the freeway, wondering about the people inside. It was strange to be only a few feet from people she'd never know. Were they happy? Glad to be heading to their destination? Or was the reason for them being on the highway filled with sadness? Or anger? Or were they thinking about the last person they killed and pondering where they'd find their next victim?

She shook off the thoughts.

"You know, I've never really thought about it before. Probably not. But maybe. I don't know…I think it depends on why I'm going on a road trip in the first place. If we're talking about this," she gestured at the black SUV, then at him, "about a work trip, I suppose I don't hate it. It's nice to get out of Chicago on someone else's dime."

Reaching into the center console for a pair of aviator sunglasses, Dean offered her an agreeable smile. In the afternoon sunlight, his whiskey-brown hair was a shade warmer and his sapphire eyes were even more vivid. "Makes sense."

"What about you? Do you like road trips?"

Dean's smile morphed into a grin. "I hate 'em. When Sherry told me she and Ted were driving all the way to the Ozarks, I thought she was screwing with me. She's supposed to be on vacation with her new hubby, but to me, a nine-hour drive sounds like she ought to be getting paid for it. I'd rather fly any day of the week."

Amelia couldn't pinpoint the reason, but his answer was unexpected. Perhaps because he was a military veteran who'd been born and raised in West Virginia and must've logged plenty of miles while in the service. Or perhaps because his tall, muscular frame evoked images of him crammed into a center seat on an airline with no room for his legs.

"Why'd you offer to drive if you hate road trips?" Amelia made no effort to hide her confusion.

"Because," Dean tapped a button on the steering wheel, his tone matter-of-fact, "if I'm driving, it means I get to pick the music."

For a beat, Dean's admission reminded Amelia of her dreadful drives with Joseph Larson.

She couldn't recall much about Dean Steelman's music preference, but there was no way in hell she was going to be subjected to the same BS Joseph Larson used to play.

Ignoring Dean's palpable confusion, she held up a hand. "Wait a second, no, that's not how this works. We live in a democracy. Either we find something we agree on, or we're listening to NPR. No further argument."

Though Amelia half expected him to be slighted by her outburst, his shoulders shook as he lapsed into a fit of laughter. Her cheeks heated as she struggled to discern whether or not he was mocking her.

"You know what? I like you, Storm. You don't take shit from anyone about anything, and I respect that." He flattened his hands against the wheel and lifted a shoulder. "For the record, I'm fine with NPR. I listened to a whole show about ducks a few weeks back. Did you know ducks have great vision? Because I didn't."

In spite of the rush of paranoia at remembering her days with Joseph Larson—the same man who'd kidnapped her sister-in-law and who'd nearly crushed her own throat—Amelia smiled. The corrupt agent was dead, having taken three shots from her hidden handgun. The tension in her shoulders lessened as the memories of Joseph passed.

Placated or not, Amelia wasn't about to risk subjecting herself to Joseph Larson's god-awful pop country. "NPR it is, then."

For the remainder of the drive, Amelia and Dean listened to a handful of different discussions on NPR, and Amelia's recollections of Joseph Larson faded. When she received a message from the Jordan County Sheriff's Office to advise that they'd dredged up yet another corpse from Lake Henrietta, the past experiences were all but forgotten.

They arrived at the sheriff's office nearly twenty minutes earlier than the GPS had estimated they would when they left Chicago. The squat sandstone building was modern, conveying an air of practicality and efficiency. After parking in the mostly empty lot, Amelia and Dean headed straight for the front doors.

As they stepped inside, a middle-aged man behind a dark wooden desk glanced up from his computer monitor. His eyes crinkled at the corners as he swiveled in his chair to face Amelia and Dean. "Hello, welcome to the Jordan County Sheriff's Office. You two must be the federal agents we've been expecting."

Amelia glanced down at her plain gray t-shirt, jeans, and boots and grinned. "How can you tell in these clothes?"

The man tapped his temple. "You can take the law enforcement officer out of the clothes, but you can't take the law enforcement out of the officer."

With Dean's plaid button-down and worn jeans, they could actually pass as residents of Henrietta City. If they hadn't both changed before departing Chicago, they'd have stuck out like a couple of sore thumbs.

They couldn't fool other LEOs, though.

Amelia retrieved her badge and identification from her back pocket. "That's true. I'm Special Agent Amelia Storm, and this is my case partner, Special Agent Dean Steelman." She was surprised she didn't have to pause before giving Dean's name. She was so used to being partnered with Zane, it was a small miracle she hadn't introduced Steelman as Zane Palmer instead.

With an easy smile, Dean flashed his badge at the deputy. "Nice to meet you. The parking lot looks a little sparse out there. I suppose everyone's out at Lake Henrietta?"

Pushing to his feet, the deputy hobbled around the desk. "That's right. Sheriff Bradley's out there with them right now too. They've got the whole place roped off to keep the public out, not that you get too many lookie-loos around here. I'm Deputy Zimmerman, by the way. But you can call me Merle."

Amelia stuck out a hand. "Nice to meet you, Deputy Zimmerman. Just wish it were under better circumstances."

"Me too." He gestured to the black boot on his right leg. "I'd rather be out there helping, but busted my ankle a couple weeks back. Wish I could say I'd been doing something interesting like snowboarding in the Rockies or surfing down in Melbourne, but I was just cleaning the gutters at my place and fell off the dang ladder. Landed wrong. Next thing you know, I'm wearing this thing."

Amelia had never cleaned a gutter in her life. Ever since she was a kid, she and her family had lived in apartments in Englewood, Chicago. Once she turned eighteen and joined the military, she'd never felt drawn enough to one place to set down roots and buy a home of her own, much less take responsibility for maintenance chores.

Dean grinned like he was a personal expert in gutter cleaning-related injuries. For all Amelia knew, he might've been. "That's how it goes sometimes."

Merle offered Dean an appreciative smile. "It does. But enough about me and my mishaps. You guys are here to help us out with the bodies we've found at Lake Henrietta, and we really appreciate it. Jordan County has a total population of about twenty-two thousand, so as you can imagine, we don't really have the specialists on staff to deal with three…no, four bodies. Especially not with the state they're in and that symbol they found."

"We're here to help." Now that the subject had moved away from cleaning gutters, Amelia was back in her element. "Have there been any updates since the last vic was discovered?"

Merle scratched his clean-shaven cheek, appearing thoughtful. "Well, the last body they found wasn't a body so much as it was a skeleton. Coroner can't say for sure how long it's been down there. Probably years. I'm thinking that's a question the experts from your lab will have to answer."

Skeletal remains were a bad sign. Typically, killers disposed of their victims in lakes and rivers to not only hide the corpse, but to wash away evidence. Amelia had dealt with one such perp over the fall, and fortunately, Lake Michigan hadn't gotten rid of *all* the trace evidence.

She doubted such a miracle would be true for the skeletal remains that had been dredged up from Lake Henrietta. Pushing aside the contemplation, she turned back to Merle. "Does the newest victim have the same symbol carved in the skull?"

The deputy nodded slowly. "They do, yeah. All four victims."

Dean's expression turned grim. "Sometimes, serial killers like to leave a signature. They're compelled to leave a mark for the crime to feel psychologically complete."

Over the handful of cases she'd worked with Dean and

his partner, Sherry Cowen, Amelia had learned that serial killers' motives rarely made any practical sense. Unlike a mob assassin, whose motive was money and power, serial killers were driven by dark urges that scientists and law enforcement officials struggled to fully understand.

Amelia still had plenty more to learn, but she was catching on fast.

The same perpetrator was responsible for the murder of all four victims, and they wanted the investigators to know it.

4

As Amelia flashed her badge at a brown-and-gold-clad deputy, she ducked beneath the yellow crime scene tape after Dean. Just as Merle had assured them, the perimeter of Lake Henrietta and the nearby woodland was roped off. Sheriff's deputies spread out across the preserve as best as they could to ensure no civilians slipped through.

Until arriving at the scene, Amelia hadn't truly appreciated how large an area they were dealing with. No way the deputies patrolling the perimeter could keep the place completely secure. But Merle had assured them that folks around Henrietta City weren't the type to trample over a crime scene. He knew the citizens around the town better than she did, so until proved otherwise, Amelia would take his word for it.

At any rate, she and Dean had plenty of work ahead of them. The Jordan County deputies had already begun searching the wooded area around the lake, but with the body count increasing, they needed all the help they could get.

Especially considering the darkening clouds looming above the horizon.

Nudging Dean's shoulder, Amelia pointed at the sky. "Looks like there's a storm coming."

He pushed his aviators to the top of his head and followed her outstretched hand. "Shit, yeah, it does." He tilted his chin toward a wooden dock, at the base of which was a veritable hive of activity. In addition to a pair of gurneys, a long, rectangular table had been set up beneath a tarp. Men and women in different uniforms and plain clothes milled about, most of them focused on their tasks and hardly aware of the arrival of the special agents.

"Let's check in with these folks. I see the forensic anthropologist over there. Looks like she beat us here."

By the time they arrived at the cluster of people, Amelia's breathing was notably heavier. Though she was five-eight and considered tall for a woman, her strides didn't eat up quite as much ground as her partner's six-three frame.

I guess I need to stop slacking on my cardio.

Catching her breath, Amelia produced her badge alongside Dean.

"Afternoon, y'all." Dean's Southern twang, which was usually subtle, intensified as he greeted the deputies and crime scene techs. He tended to use it as a way to ingratiate the Bureau outsiders with the locals. As he rattled off an introduction, a woman wearing a brown ball cap with a gold sheriff's star appeared visibly relieved.

"Agents, I'm so glad you're here." Snapping off a vinyl glove, she swiped at her forehead. "I'm Sheriff Rhonda Bradley." She gestured at a short bald man standing beside a pair of gurneys. "This is the Jordan County coroner, Reggie Hoffman. Reggie was just giving your Dr. Islas a rundown of the victims we've found so far. There are these two here, which are the two who've been dead longer. The two victims killed more recently were taken back to the morgue so we could preserve them until we send them all to Cook County."

Clipboard in one gloved hand, Reggie gave a slight wave with the other.

At his side, Dr. Alicia Islas acknowledged their arrival with a nod, appearing as if she were just another hiker out for a stroll. Her wide-brimmed hat kept the sun from her face, and her t-shirt, jeans, and black calf-high boots were far more practical for the environment than a lab coat would've been. The anthropologist's ebony hair and tanned skin contrasted against Reggie's pale complexion. Amelia realized the man likely spent much of his time in the morgue.

Sheriff Bradley waved a hand toward a pair of divers seated at the rocky shore of the lake. "The divers are both trained underwater crime scene investigators from the state police department. We called them in after a Henrietta City local found the first body while he was out on the water fishing yesterday evening. The divers are taking a short break before they go back in. Meanwhile, our priority is searching the area around the lake. This isn't officially a campground, but it's well-known enough to folks around here who like to brave the great outdoors."

Amelia scanned the expansive lake. Though the body of water was too large for her to make out specific details of the opposite shore, she spotted no movement. Fortunately, not all the area surrounding the lake was woodland. They still had a great deal of ground to cover, though, and judging by the encroaching storm clouds, they might not have much time to beat the weather.

"We've got the area taped off as best we can. We've also got some of our friends from the Carroll County Sheriff's Office helping with the search." The sheriff's voice returned Amelia's gaze to the gathering. "I've got a couple of my team posted at the entrances. They're turning people away, but we haven't made an official statement to the media. We figured the Bureau would want to be involved in that."

The more Amelia learned about the vastness of the undertaking, the more sense it made to her that Sheriff Bradley would reach out to the FBI so quickly. Not only did the Bureau have specialists trained to deal with unique cases, it also offered additional bodies to help cover the vast expanse of the nature preserve. And with an impending storm lurking in the distance, every minute counted to gather any potential evidence before it was washed away.

5
———

Amelia exchanged a quick glance with Dean. His determined expression told her they were on the same page. "Thank you, Sheriff. Let us catch up with the medical examiner and Dr. Islas, and then we'll be ready to help with the search."

Sheriff Bradley pulled off her other glove and nodded. "Okay, just give me the word, and I'll radio a couple of my team down to show you around and help get you up to speed. I'm going to check and see what the game plan is for our divers."

As the sheriff headed down toward the dock, Amelia took note of the table where two crime scene techs were parsing through and bagging evidence. She followed Dean over to a nearby pair of gurneys.

"What've we got so far?" Dean gestured to the flatter of the two body bags. "Deputy Zimmerman told us the victim y'all found while we were on our way here was just a collection of bones."

"Sure is." The coroner hung his clipboard on the side of the gurney, beckoning the forensic anthropologist to come closer as he reached for the zipper. "The divers had to make a few trips back and forth to transfer all the bones. They photographed the site where they found the skeleton."

Peering down at the bones arranged on the black material of the body bag, Amelia wondered how long it would take the divers to finish a search of the whole lake. The water didn't seem dirty, but it wasn't crystal clear either. "We'll get ahold of our office and see who they can send to help with the underwater search. There might be some technology they can provide too."

"Good call." Dean beamed her an appreciative smile before turning back to the forensic anthropologist. "Nice to see you again, Dr. Islas, even though I wish it were for better reasons."

Dean and Amelia had first encountered the doctor and her team when they worked on the case of the Fox Creek Butcher. She'd been an asset then, and Amelia was confident the woman's knowledge would prove useful again.

The forensic anthropologist lifted her shoulder. "Well, in our line of work, there really aren't many other circumstances."

"Fair point." Dean nodded at the collection of bones. "Anything you can tell us about the victim so far?"

"A little." Dr. Islas produced a pair of vinyl gloves, snapping them on before she reached for the stained skull. "Other than being worn down by the water and the elements, the victim's skull is relatively intact. All the teeth are in place, so we should be able to get a dental imprint once she's back at the lab."

Amelia's eyebrow shot up of its own accord. "She?"

"Correct. I had a chance to look over Jane Doe's skeleton before you arrived. Based on the shape of her pelvis, along with some distinguishing features of her skull, I'm confident these remains are those of a woman."

She paused to tip the skull backward in her hands, revealing a strange, jagged symbol carved into the bone.

An eerie chill crawled down Amelia's back at the sight. Sure, she'd experienced her share of gruesome crime scenes. More than her fair share, in fact. But the act of etching a symbol into the bones of a murder victim made for a grim spectacle.

The forensic anthropologist's voice cut through her contemplation. "I'm not sure what this symbol means, but we'll run it through the Bureau's databases and see if it lines up with a gang or a cult or some other type of criminal group."

Amelia held back a laugh. It would be just her luck to transfer to Violent Crimes only to have her first case be connected to the Mob.

Hovering her finger along a squiggly line that ran along the top of the skull, Dr. Islas glanced at Amelia and Dean. "I believe I discussed cranial sutures with Agent Cowen on the last case we worked together."

Amelia recalled the notes Sherry had made for the case around last Thanksgiving. "Sorry, but you may need to bring us up to speed."

Dr. Islas smiled. "That's no problem. The more the sutures are fused together, the older the person. Based on Jane Doe's cranial sutures, I can tell you she was a young woman, probably in her twenties. I'll be able to get a better estimate on her age and ethnicity in the lab."

Crossing his arms, Dean surveyed the skeletal remains. "This is probably a long shot, but do you have any idea what killed her?"

The anthropologist turned the skull around to show

them the back of the victim's head. "I can't say for sure this was the cause of death without closer examination, but this wound would be my current hypothesis." She pointed at a puncture wound at the base of the skull. "Whatever it was, *possibly* a bullet, though I hesitate to confirm that, it struck her from behind. There's no damage to any bones on the front of the skull, although it is possible the projectile could've entered through soft tissue such as the eye."

Dean swatted at a fly and scrunched up his nose at the bug's intrusion.

"The mark is angled slightly downward." Dr. Islas followed the angle with a fingertip. "I don't think a bullet would do that unless fired from an elevated spot such as a hunting blind. But the hole isn't big enough nor is the damage extensive enough to the surrounding structures for it to have been caused by a bullet. I don't think. It's hard to tell what exactly caused the injury. The medical examiner will know more about that when her remains are transferred to Cook County."

Leaning closer, Amelia inspected the small hole. "Yeah, I see it. Could the perp have been standing above her?"

"It's possible." Dr. Islas returned the skull to the gurney. "There's no exit wound that I can see. Closer examination should show the projectile's path through the skull."

Amelia knew it would be unlikely, but she had to ask. "Any idea about time of death?"

Dr. Islas sighed. "Aquatic taphonomy complicates things. When remains are submerged, water introduces a range of variables that affect decomposition. Water temperature, oxygen content, and even the aquatic life present can all alter the rate at which a body breaks down."

Amelia mentally cursed, even though she'd known the answer. "Any guesses?"

The doctor wrinkled her nose. "Factors like scavenger marks, bone-staining from minerals, or encrustation by marine organisms will provide clues. Initial indications suggest the remains have been there for more than a year. To give you a more precise timeline, I'll need to conduct a lab examination."

Dean was bent low, still studying the skull. "Okay, so we can rule out a high-powered rifle. There'd be a hell of a lot more damage if she'd been hit with a rifle, or even a close shot from most handguns."

Amelia glanced at the forensic anthropologist. "I know the other Jane Doe is back at the morgue to preserve as much of her as possible. Is it your opinion that she's only been dead for a couple days? Does she have the same wound as this Jane Doe?"

Dr. Islas zipped the black bag closed over the skeleton on the first gurney. "I had a chance to look at her briefly before she was transported. The wound was not the same. Her throat was slit, and the cut was so deep, it nearly decapitated her. And..." she paused, shifting her weight from one foot to the other, "the same symbol is carved in her skull. Before she was scalped."

Though the announcement didn't come as a surprise to Amelia—she and Dean had already theorized how the perpetrator would have gone about carving a symbol into their victims' skulls—hearing the statement spoken out loud made the scenario even more unnerving.

Whoever the killer was, there was no doubt about their intent.

They were on a mission.

And if they weren't caught soon, they *would* kill again.

6

Ducking beneath a low-hanging branch, Dean swiped away the sheen of perspiration built up on his forehead. The temperature had barely broken eighty degrees, but the forested area around Lake Henrietta stifled any breeze. He'd been hiking through the woods for the past thirty-five minutes, and so far, all he'd accomplished was working up a sweat.

For as small as the Jordan County Sheriff's Office was, their team was organized. They'd assigned him and Amelia each their own section of the search grid. In addition to evidence flags, he and Amelia had each taken a camera so they could photograph any places or items of interest.

According to Deputy Jonah Hester—the young man who'd gone over the search progress with Dean and Amelia before they were given their own areas to conquer—search and rescue operations weren't terribly uncommon. Any place with hiking trails and campgrounds came with the risk of civilians getting lost. Usually, the deputies were looking for a kid separated from their family or a hiker who'd gotten turned around.

Not for clues about who might have committed four murders.

As Dean made his way toward an especially tall oak, the quiet crackle of dried brush froze him in place. Goose bumps worked their way down his back like the skittering of a cluster of spiders.

What the hell was that? Deputy Hester? Shouldn't he be working the grid east of me?

Though Dean was certain the noise hadn't come from him, he glanced down to where he'd stopped just shy of one of the oak's exposed roots. A few leaves lay upon the ground, but none of them were dried, and the small amount of grass and weeds pushing through the earth was green and fresh.

Not that any of that mattered. He'd heard the direction of the sound, which sure as hell wasn't from under his foot.

One hand inching closer to the service weapon holstered beneath his plaid shirt, he whipped his head around to check the direction from which the noise had come. All the while, the chattering of birds, critters, and insects continued, unconcerned with the matter.

Maybe nothing happened. Maybe I'm losing my mind.

"Don't be stupid," he reminded himself.

Back during his days in the military, he'd learned an important lesson. When he was behind enemy lines, there was no such thing as being too paranoid. Hyperawareness had saved his life overseas more times than he could count, and that vigilance had served him just as well during his decade with the Bureau.

Chances were the sound had been made either by an animal or a deputy who'd wandered too far away from their own search grid. Those were the rational explanations, and Dean wasn't about to start his newest case by accidentally shooting one of the Jordan County deputies.

Clearing his throat, he swiveled his head to take in the rest of the area. "Hello? Anyone there?"

A bird squawked in the tree above him, but otherwise, the scene was quiet.

"Great. Guess I'm getting spooked by a possum or something."

Possums and raccoons are nocturnal.

"Okay, then maybe it was a deer. Take your pick, all right?"

Now he was arguing with himself. How productive.

Rubbing his forehead with the back of one hand, Dean gritted his teeth and did his best to shake off the baseless anxiety. Nothing good would come from him reliving the same paranoia that had followed him from the Battle of Fallujah and throughout the Middle East.

Gingerly, he started to pick his way around the massive oak. He wasn't about to ignore his hypervigilance entirely, but he also had a job to do. The good news was that he'd been trained by the U.S. government on how to watch his own ass *and* do his job. Though, his view was obscured beneath the trees, he could still tell the storm clouds were moving closer.

As Dean passed the massive oak, a splash of an unnatural hue caught his eye. The shade of blue was seldom spotted in nature and sure wasn't something found in the Illinois woods.

With a quick glance over his shoulder to reassure himself he wasn't being followed, Dean increased his pace as he neared the royal blue pop of color. From a distance, the splotch was obscured by tree branches and foliage. Careful to mind his steps lest he trip on a tree root or a rock, he closed in on what he now realized was a small clearing.

Excitement shot through him like a firecracker. The mysterious blue item was a *tent*.

Recalling the incident that had startled him only minutes earlier, Dean eased his hand closer to his service weapon.

"Excuse me, is anyone there?" His voice seemed to echo back at him, and even though there was a veritable squad of sheriff's deputies and crime scene techs nearby, he was struck by an acute sense of isolation.

Pausing at the edge of the clearing, he surveyed the campsite.

The tent appeared to have lost a battle with a bear. Broad slashes crisscrossed the nylon material, and the fabric near the hole had drooped without support.

What the hell?

He instinctively crouched lower and scanned the trees, straining for any sounds. Nothing. Yet he couldn't shake the feeling he was being watched. Stepping into the clearing would make him an easy target.

When Dean moved around a few trees at the edge of the clearing to secure a better vantage point, the campsite came more fully into view. A circle of stones once containing a fire was now ashes and blackened wood. A small cooler sat in the grass near the tent, along with a cast-iron pan, two mugs, and a few cooking supplies. Whoever had set up the tent and the makeshift cooking ring had been settled in.

"Hello?" Dean held still as he waited for a response, paying close attention to his periphery to spot—or hear—any hint of movement.

The spiders' legs were back. He didn't suffer from the side effects of hypervigilance much, but the eerie sensation of someone else nearby, someone hidden, wouldn't leave him. All the deputies he'd met so far were polite but mostly stone-faced and task-oriented. Dean sincerely doubted one of those men or women would leave their post just to screw with him.

Is it the killer?

His mouth went dry, but he had to admit, he hoped it was. Better for him to confront the bastard now with backup only seconds away than risk them killing another person.

Closing one hand around the grip of his service weapon, Dean took the first step out of the trees and into the clearing. "This is Agent Steelman with the Federal Bureau of Investigation. If anyone's here, identify yourself and come out with your hands where I can see them."

He half expected a burly man with an unkempt beard to emerge from the woods with a club.

Birds chattered overhead. A couple of squirrels raced up a tree on the other side of the clearing.

Satisfied there was no one in the open area, Dean advanced toward the tent, carefully choosing his steps to avoid trampling any potential evidence.

As he came to the front, he finally relinquished his grip on his Glock. Reaching for the camera dangling around his neck, he knelt to get a better view of the tent's destruction.

The zip-up doorway was shredded to ribbons. And with the way the material was pushed outward, he suspected the person who'd carved up the doorway had been inside the tent. But why not just unzip the flap?

The uncomfortable feeling of someone watching him grew, reminding him of every horror movie he'd ever seen in his thirty-seven years of life.

Why couldn't he shake that impression?

7

Dean checked over his shoulder for what had to have been the hundredth time, but yet again, there was no movement. Setting aside the rampant paranoia, he returned his focus to the bizarre scene in front of him.

Could the damage to the tent have been caused by an animal? No, not unless the animal had somehow gotten caught inside the tent and tried to claw its way free. After all, the tent's door flap had shards of fabric facing outward.

Zooming in on the damage, Dean snapped a series of photos. The crime scene techs would do the same once they arrived at the site, but there was something about taking the pictures himself that helped him believe he was making progress on a case, even if that was simply documenting a scene to pore over later on.

He'd just reached for his radio to call in his find when a voice reached him.

"Agent Steelman?"

With his focus ripped away from the strange campsite, Dean gripped his weapon tighter. "Who's there?"

"Deputy Hester." Brush and leaves crackled.

Dean relaxed a little. "Watch your step. I think this is the site of the attack."

"Really?" Excitement tinged Hester's response. As the young man skirted the edge of the clearing, he paused to gesture to the side of the tent Dean had noticed earlier. "Jeez, it's like someone was trying to rip another opening into this thing."

"I know. And there are more cuts on the door flap."

Both men stared at the destroyed canvas, which had been ripped wide open, the flap rustling faintly in the breeze.

Dean raised the camera and took another series of photos. "The front opening appears to have been cut from the inside."

Readjusting his ball cap, Hester turned to Dean. With his bright eyes and clean-shaven face, the deputy could've passed for a high schooler. "Inside?"

"Yeah. The marks are neat, just like these larger ones on the other end. Looks like someone made 'em with a blade. The ones on the door are pushed outward and the ones on the back have flopped inward. I think they were made by two different blades and possibly two different people."

Hester pointed at the gash in the tent side, his expression contemplative. "Have you ever heard of the Dyatlov Pass Incident?"

"It sounds familiar. Why?"

"Well, it was this group of hikers in Russia. They were...I don't know, going on some sort of winter wilderness trip."

"They were hiking? In Russia, during the winter?" Just the thought baffled Dean. "I'm sure that ended well."

"About as well as you'd expect. They left for their trip and never came back. It was weeks before search parties found them, and by then, they were long dead. But one thing the Russian investigators noticed, and one thing that's always brought up when I watch something about it, was that the people cut their way out of their tents. Like they were so desperate to get away from something that they didn't even try to use the zipper."

There was no mistaking the parallels between the Dyatlov Pass Incident and the partially destroyed tent. "All right, yeah. I see it. So then, one theory is that whoever was inside the tent was more than likely trying to get away from someone on the outside. But I don't understand why the attacker would allow the camper to leave."

With a shrug, Hester pushed back his hat enough to scratch his forehead, destroying what little good his earlier readjustment had done. "Beats me."

Dean turned back toward Deputy Hester. "I'm going to take some more pictures and see what the evidence tells me. And I want to get a closer look at the zipper to see why they didn't use that. I'm betting it might've jammed or it was too dark to see. Could you get ahold of the sheriff and let her know what we found? See if Agent Storm and one of the crime scene techs can get over here to take a look at this."

"No problem. I'm on it." Hester reached for his radio.

Dean nodded his thanks. "We still have a lot of questions to answer, but I have an idea this tent and the bodies in the lake are connected."

8

Upon her arrival at the campsite, Amelia figured she now knew what miners experienced when they struck gold for the first time. With the threat of a storm growing ever closer, two of the crime scene techs had quickly gotten to work, splitting the clearing in half. Already, they'd brought tarps to put up to preserve what they could before the rain began to fall.

So far, in addition to the items present at the campsite, a few shoe imprints leading toward the front of the tent had been marked. To Amelia's chagrin, the tent itself had been erected on a patch of ground completely covered in grass, so they were unlikely to get additional usable prints from the area. Amelia and Dean had both concluded their presence would crowd the clearing and impede the ability of the CSU to do their job quickly and efficiently, so they stood together at the edge of the clearing.

Considering the handful of tracks present in the dried dirt, Sheriff Bradley had called in the help of an expert tracker from neighboring Carroll County. The deputy typically specialized in tracking for search and rescue missions, but she'd also aided in murder investigations in the past.

Which meant, as much as Amelia wanted to help move along the process, she was stuck waiting. Neither she nor Dean wanted to leave the immediate area lest they miss out on a discovery that could help steer the investigation.

At her side, the same impatience practically rolled off her new partner. If they didn't find a task to do soon, she suspected they might both lose their minds.

As Amelia was about to open her mouth to ask him for his thoughts so far, one of the two techs—a middle-aged woman named Patsy Wilkerson—stepped away from the royal blue tent. Turning toward the agents, she held out a gloved hand to beckon them over. "I think I've got something for you. Come take a look."

Amelia was more than happy to oblige. With Dean right on her heels, she picked her way past a marked set of shoe prints to where Wilkerson was posted by the tent. "What is it?"

"Wallets. Here. They were inside this backpack." The tech retrieved two sets of vinyl gloves from her kit and handed them to Amelia and Dean.

Tugging on the gloves, Amelia kept her anticipation in check as Wilkerson held out a leather wallet.

Before Amelia could comment, Wilkerson offered a second clear-plastic waterproof wallet from the pack. "I've still got to go through everything in the backpack and photograph it, but I thought you'd want to see these for yourselves. I took a quick look, and there are IDs inside. Iowa driver's licenses."

Amelia flipped open the clear wallet and, sure enough, found the license tucked behind a clear pane of plastic.

"Jeremy Fitzgerald. Address listed here is for Waterloo, Iowa. He's...twenty-three years old."

"Leslie Armstrong, twenty-two, turns twenty-three next month." Dean held out the tan leather wallet so Amelia could get a better look at the license. "She look familiar to you?"

When Amelia peered down at the image of a young woman staring blankly into a camera at the DMV, recognition ignited. "Yeah, she does. She looked different in the crime scene photos, but that's her. That's the first Jane Doe they pulled out of the lake."

Dean nodded. "Yep, that's her. Her school ID is in here too. It was issued about four years ago, so she was probably going to graduate soon." He paused to gesture to the wallet in Amelia's hands. "I reckon the John Doe from the crime scene photos is Jeremy."

Amelia's stomach sank as she looked back at Jeremy Fitzgerald's license. Her partner was right.

Turning to Patsy Wilkerson, Amelia held out the wallet. "Could you take a photo of this license and make sure it gets added to the case file?"

Patsy collected the wallets and deposited them into evidence bags. "Yeah, I can do that."

A pair of voices nearing the scene drew their collective attention.

Sheriff Bradley emerged beside the trunk of a tall maple just outside the clearing, followed closely by a younger woman in a blue-and-black Carroll County Sheriff's Department uniform. As her light-brown eyes met Amelia's, a smile creased her face. "Thank you for waiting."

Returning the smile, Amelia made her way to the sheriff and her companion. "No problem."

Before Amelia could ask a follow-up question, Sheriff

Bradley gestured to the younger woman. "This is Deputy Avery Foveaux. She's trained in tracking humans and animals. Usually, she helps us with search and rescue, but she's helped with a few homicide investigations too."

Amelia glanced around. "Where's your dog?"

Foveaux grinned. "It's just me."

This was going to be interesting. "Sorry. When I hear 'tracking,' I automatically think of sniffer dogs."

Her grin grew wider. "You're not the first. And from what I've heard, there are a few dogs on the way, but right now," she raised her nose to the air and sniffed, "you've got me."

With a distracted nod, the sheriff bade them good luck before setting off toward the lake. The woman was running around like a chicken with her head cut off, and Amelia was more than grateful for all her efforts. Though the FBI was taking over the investigation, the local deputies were far more likely to listen to their sheriff than a couple federal agents from the big city.

Besides, the managerial role had never been Amelia's cup of tea. She'd once overheard her previous boss, former Supervisory Special Agent Spencer Corsaw, compare his work to herding cats. If Hup was any indication, Amelia wanted no part of that sideshow.

Thank the sheriff later. Time to get to work.

Amelia glanced toward the encroaching clouds. "It's hard to say how much time we've got before the storm gets here, but we should work quickly."

Dean jerked a thumb toward the campsite. "I can stay here to help the CSU bag evidence and get this area processed. Doubt I'd be much help stumbling through these woods anyway."

Deputy Foveaux grinned. "Tracking isn't as difficult as it

seems. But you're right, Agent Storm. We should get started."

Amelia wasn't sure the task was as easy as Foveaux thought, but she was looking forward to the introduction to a new skill.

9

After grabbing her camera and a backpack full of supplies—flags to mark places of interest, angled rulers for any photos she took, evidence collection supplies, and a few other basic forensic tools she was trained to use—Amelia led Deputy Avery Foveaux to the point of origin, the royal blue tent. While the woman checked over the area, carefully observing the sites around each evidence marker, Amelia stood to the side and observed.

The deputy gestured at the grassy patch of ground where the tent had been erected. "That grass is thick enough that it didn't hold any prints, but the area around the firepit over here is interesting. See, there are a lot of prints in this general location. Two different sources, at least to start with. I'd be willing to bet they belong to the campers who were here. But then, there's another, larger set of prints that seems to come from that direction," she gestured toward the woods away from the tent, "and heads toward the side of the tent."

Shifting her weight from one foot to the other, Amelia followed the deputy's movements as the woman crept toward the ruined flap of the tent, then to the side with the larger, longer gashes. The entire scene had already been documented and was being processed by the CSU. Though Amelia wanted to move on, she reminded herself the deputy needed to establish a baseline—a context for her search.

Amelia gestured to the shredded door flap. "We're thinking that's where the victims fled the tent. We've confirmed the cuts were made from the inside."

"Right." Deputy Foveaux pointed toward a gap between a pair of trees. "More than likely, after getting out of the tent, they'd have headed straight for the woods. This spot seems like the obvious choice."

Wordlessly, Amelia followed the woman, her camera at the ready.

For the next ten to twenty minutes, she carefully shadowed Deputy Foveaux. Amelia took photos regularly—placing a ruler near objects of interest for scale—but she relied on the deputy to tell her when a part of the trail was worth closer observation. Foveaux explained her reasoning each time they changed direction as she pointed out broken branches, crushed leaves, and plenty of other breadcrumbs.

Amelia understood the gist of tracking, but with each subsequent clue, she gained a deeper understanding of this foreign language. She wasn't fluent yet, however, so the deputy's unwavering confidence was reassuring.

Pausing in front of a stump overgrown with weeds, Deputy Foveaux glanced back at Amelia. "It looks like the campers got separated here. One set of prints goes that way, to the northwest, and the other continues northeast." She pressed her lips together. "And they were likely running."

Amelia squatted to inspect the print better. "Is that from the length of the stride?"

"Nice. Yes, that and the depth of the impression and

pattern of contact to start. We'll need to study the orientation more closely, but that's my initial impression."

If two people were running for their lives in the middle of the night, Amelia could easily picture them getting split up somewhere along the way. "How about the larger set of prints? The ones we think might belong to the person who chased them out of that camp?"

Lips pursed, Foveaux crept around the stump, her focus glued to the ground. "Well, we're a little lucky, because there's a patch of dried dirt here. The larger prints head northeast, following the smaller of the two campers."

"Leslie Armstrong. Her license said she was five-three." Taking her cue, Amelia readied the camera and retrieved a yellow evidence flag.

Once she finished documenting the spot and making a note of its location in her notebook, Deputy Foveaux strode toward the northeast.

It wasn't long before they spotted a piece of pastel-blue fabric on the end of a broken, low-hanging branch. Hurrying to beat the storm, Amelia snapped a series of pictures before tagging the location and bagging the item.

"It doesn't look like there was a confrontation here." Foveaux rested her hands on her hips and scanned the trees.

"Looks to me like the victim, probably Leslie Armstrong, hit this branch while she was running." Amelia tested the knowledge she'd been acquiring since they left the clearing with the tent.

"Right. The larger footprints are still following her, but if those prints belong to the perp, he could've been some distance behind her."

The assertion painted a grim picture of Leslie's fight to survive.

"So he was stalking her while she ran for her life?"

"Based on the pattern and depth of both sets of impressions, yes. She was running, and he was walking."

Had the perp wanted to catch Leslie specifically? Why had he followed her and not Jeremy? When outnumbered, most assailants took out the biggest threat first, which was definitely Jeremy, based on the physical description on his driver's license.

Amelia set the questions on the back burner of her mind. They'd puzzle through the photos and evidence later. Right now, they had a storm to beat.

Deputy Foveaux switched her focus to the woods. Gradually, as they moved deeper between tree trunks, the babble of running water grew more distinct. Amelia didn't have to be an expert tracker to recognize they were headed toward a river.

Just like the victim had done on the night she was killed.

Pausing beside a birch, Deputy Foveaux glanced at Amelia before gesturing at an upcoming clearing. "Both prints lead this way."

Amelia put down a handful of evidence flags, snapped a few more pictures, and followed the deputy out of the trees. The patch of grassy earth was larger than she'd expected, probably used by numerous past campers.

As Amelia scanned the area, she halted in place. Less than ten feet away from the tree line, the vivid green of the grass was stained by a large, dark splotch. Anticipation thrummed in her chest like the notes of a well-tuned piano.

She patted Foveaux's arm. "Nice nose."

Because the hue of dried blood was unmistakable.

10

In the span of fifteen minutes, the clearing beside the river went from isolated and peaceful to Grand Central Station. Amelia remained in the midst of the action the entire time. If she wasn't taking pictures, she was helping the CSU bring in equipment and tarps. Anything she could do to help move the operation along.

Fortunately, the techs at the campsite had already set up a shelter for their scene, so they came to help with the newest discovery.

After handing over a couple of PVC poles, Amelia spotted Dean standing near the trees, a bottle of water in hand. She'd been so busy working with the CSU and Deputy Foveaux, she hadn't realized how thirsty she was. Pulling an unopened bottle from the mesh side pocket of her backpack, she waved to him and made her way over.

"Hey, Storm. Nice work." He twisted the cap back onto his water.

"Oh, no. I'm not going to pretend to take credit for that. I've learned a lot, but Deputy Foveaux is the one who did all the work. I just operated the camera, collected evidence, and hazarded a few educated guesses." Amelia took her first sip of water. Though it had long since warmed to room temperature, the drink was just as refreshing as an icy beverage.

He chuckled. "Well, either way, good work. Sounds like you got a crash course in Tracking 101." He gestured at the pair of dried blood stains in the center of the clearing. "What do you make of everything so far? Looks to me like those kids were ambushed in the middle of the night."

"Yeah, I think so. They got split up while they were running through the woods, but they might've done it on purpose. If they were being chased by an assailant, they could've decided to split up so at least one of them would have better odds of escaping." Amelia wasn't quite sure how her hypothesis held up under scrutiny, but she still acknowledged it as a possibility.

Dean's nod was noncommittal, and Amelia suspected he also harbored doubts. "Right. Could've been a split-second decision. Not like they'd have had time to plan anything if they were taken by surprise while they were sleeping."

"That reminds me. They were both wearing shoes. Is that…normal? For people camping and sleeping in a tent?"

Appearing thoughtful, Dean picked at the label on his bottle of water. "Honestly? You're asking the wrong guy. I appreciate the amenities a cabin offers, you know? I stayed in plenty of tents when I was a kid, but I couldn't tell you if I slept with my shoes on. It makes sense, though, doesn't it? It's what we did in the military."

Memories of nights spent on the cold hard ground made Amelia's back ache. "Yeah, but that was because we were in a combat zone. And because it's the military, you've got to be ready for anything." Then again, if Amelia and Zane were spending the night in a tent—an idea that made Amelia's city slicker brain misfire—she could picture herself wearing shoes to bed.

Dean waved a dismissive hand. "Point is, it's entirely possible both vics slept with their shoes on." He turned his focus to the pair of trees where Leslie had exited the woods. "Okay, so, Leslie Armstrong makes it to the clearing over there, but the perp is still following her. Do you think she'd run into a clearing if she knew the guy was right on her heels?"

"That depends. Did she even *know* she was running into a clearing? She might've realized it too late, and with the perp behind her, she didn't have the option to change course and run back into the woods to try to lose him."

"Very true. Now, when she gets here, she runs toward the river. She realizes she's hit a dead end, and she probably knows the guy is stalking right behind her by now. Then she's got a choice to make. Does she risk jumping into the river to get away from him, or does she keep running even though he knows where she is?"

Amelia raised a hand. "We've got to keep in mind that she's not in a position to make the soundest, most logical choice. She's just woken up, she's terrified, and her body is surging with adrenaline. Adrenaline always turns people into superheroes on TV, but in the real world, it can screw you up as much as it can help you. Especially if you're not used to high levels of it."

Turning toward the twin blood stains, Dean scratched his cheek. "Based on the way the grass was trampled, plus the copious amounts of blood on the ground, the vics were killed right there. We've got what we assume are Leslie's footprints leading to the blood on the right and Jeremy's prints leading to the stain on the left. But the perp with the big feet from the campsite only seems to have followed

Leslie. I'm not sure what that means for Jeremy or when he got here."

He had a point. After Jeremy and Leslie got separated in the woods, it was a crapshoot to determine the time when they each separately emerged in the clearing.

"Well, Deputy Foveaux is tracing Jeremy's footprints to find the path he took, and she's going to check the other half of the clearing for anything there that'll answer our questions. Based on what I learned as we followed Leslie's tracks, there were only two sets of prints. Unless Jeremy was swinging through the trees like Tarzan, he wasn't with Leslie when she arrived here."

Dean's expression turned curious. "Maybe Jeremy showed up midway through Leslie's confrontation with the killer, or..." He studied the blood stains before looking back at Amelia. "Maybe the killer tracked Leslie, waited, then ambushed them both."

Though Amelia's knee-jerk reaction was to point out how that would mean the perp willingly subjected himself to a two-versus-one scenario, she reminded herself of the size of the man's footprints. Would five-three, one-hundred-pound Leslie Armstrong and five-nine, one-hundred-sixty-pound Jeremy Fitzgerald have been a match for a large, potentially muscular man wielding a blade?

Other than the knife used to slice their way out of the tent, it was likely Jeremy and Leslie were unarmed.

"Yeah, that's plausible." Amelia took a deep drink from her water, ignoring the grumbling in her stomach. If she didn't get her hands on caffeine and food soon, she'd turn into a zombie.

"Agents! You're going to want to see this."

11

Amelia's attention snapped away from her hungry stomach at Deputy Foveaux's emphatic call.

Cheeks flushed from exertion, Foveaux trotted toward them along the edge of the clearing.

Amelia twisted the cap back on her water and headed her way. "Did something happen? Did you find something?"

Stopping just in front of Amelia and Dean, Deputy Foveaux took a deep breath and nodded. "Yes. Over there, not far from where we found Jeremy's tracks." She pointed at a thicket of trees at the other end of the clearing. "There's another set of footprints. Those are smaller than the impressions left by the person who ambushed the campsite."

"Wait, a fourth set of prints?" Amelia glanced up at the darkening sky, her pulse drumming in her ears. "All right, let's take a look. We've got to work quickly." Like a pop quiz in school, Amelia's education was about to be put to the test.

"Right. Come on."

As Amelia powered on her camera, she and Dean

hurried after the deputy, careful to avoid the section of the clearing under examination by the CSU.

Jogging toward the line of trees, Foveaux beckoned the agents closer. "Here. There's a spot of dirt right by this maple that was soft enough to get a good impression."

Dean flashed Foveaux a quick thumbs-up. "Storm, I'll leave you and the deputy to it. I'm going to grab a tech to make a cast of this print."

Amelia offered him a casual salute. "Aye-aye, partner."

A flicker of amusement passed over Dean's face before he turned and made his way back to the CSU.

"All right, let's mark this." Amelia produced a yellow flag and handed it to Deputy Foveaux. "Could this be an earlier impression left by Leslie?"

"No, I don't think so." Crouching beside the tree, Foveaux pointed to the faint pattern of a tread. "Leslie Armstrong was wearing sneakers, and this is a print from a boot."

What if Leslie was wearing boots earlier in the day? No, that doesn't make sense. There was no footwear discovered at the couple's camp, based on the itemized list the techs compiled.

Foveaux must have sensed Amelia's skepticism. "This print is also a couple sizes larger than Leslie's, at least." She rose to her full height, gazing into the woods. "I followed the tracks into the trees a ways, and, well...it looks like they were mirroring Jeremy's."

"A second stalker?"

"That's the explanation that makes the most sense. But it's possible these tracks are older than the two victims' tracks."

Amelia caught the caveat. "But that wouldn't explain why they were mirroring Jeremy's. It's too much of a coincidence. That means we're looking for two perps."

"Yeah, that's my conclusion. It'll be a little more difficult to differentiate between the tracks on the grass, but these tracks are headed this way." She waved a hand in the direction of the bloodstains.

"Let's see if we can figure it out. We don't have much time before the rain hits." When Amelia pulled in a calming breath, the scent of rain was more prominent. She gestured in a semicircle. "It looks like they stayed on the outskirts of the scuffle that happened near the blood."

Foveaux smiled. "Maybe I'll just have a seat over there while you keep tracking. You're pretty good at this."

"Ha. I'm not letting you get away that easily." As Amelia conjured a mental image of her hypothesis, she was reminded of a big cat circling its prey. "It's like this person was patrolling. Or…maybe they got here afterward, and they were surveying the scene?"

"Could be. If they were an onlooker, or if they were someone who got here after the fact, why wouldn't they call the cops?"

"Good point. If that's the case, then it means they either don't want to be found, or they're complicit." A rumble of thunder jerked Amelia's gaze upward. The afternoon sky had grown much darker. "Shit. Okay. I'll call Agent Steelman and have him corral a tech to come photograph this whole area while you and I follow these tracks before the storm hits."

Foveaux nodded. "Perfect."

Based on what Amelia had combed through so far, she was confident they could spend days out here in the woods searching for clues and puzzle over the handful of tracks. If they weren't about to be interrupted by a thunderstorm, they'd have done just that.

Her only option now was to gather as much new evidence as possible and hope it'd be enough. And that they weren't about to lose some vital clue to Mother Nature.

12

Though I'd been gone from the hospital for nearly two hours, the stench of sickness and death still clung to me. Nearly three weeks after my mother's stroke, and I was still expected to visit and care for the old bat.

It was a shame the stroke hadn't taken her ability to speak or, even better, killed her altogether. Having to deal with the hospital staff, play the part of the grieving daughter, and waste hours of my day traveling back and forth to the hospital...I deserved an Emmy for this shit. Maybe even a Nobel Prize.

I pushed aside my thoughts and considered the circular staircase at the other end of the living room. The entire foyer was cloaked in soft shadow, with blue light from the pool outside shimmering along the hardwood floor near the windows that lined the back of the house.

The end of April seemed too early to fill the pool, but my husband had taken matters into his own hands as soon as temperatures hit the mid-eighties. Opening the pool early was the least of my grievances with that man.

Scoffing, I turned away from the stairs. I could shower

off this godforsaken stench after I finished my nightly target practice. Ever since I'd missed a shot during my last hunt, I'd committed to preventing the same mistake from happening in the future.

My brother's incessant teasing hadn't helped matters. He'd been there. He'd witnessed that stupid college kid shift to the side to dodge my shot. It was out of my control.

Not like he could've landed a better shot. There was a reason he used that machete. He couldn't hit the broad side of a barn with my crossbow.

Recalling his smug smile breathed life into the fires of determination in my gut. As I neared the end of the short hall leading to my indoor archery range, I rolled my shoulders and entered a six-digit code into the keypad beside the door. With a metallic *click*, the lock disengaged, and I let myself in.

I got to work right away, switching on lights to illuminate the range as well as the counter and storage behind it. Crossbows and compound bows hung from the wall, neatly arranged by size and shape. No one other than my brother and me were ever back here, but I still maintained some semblance of class.

After retrieving a plastic container of bolts and my favorite crossbow, I pulled open a drawer beneath the counter. A ripple of grim satisfaction rolled over me as my gaze settled on a stack of glossy photo prints.

From where she lay on her death bed in the hospital, my mother hardly resembled the poised, stone-faced woman in the pictures. The photos had been taken on her and my father's forty-fifth wedding anniversary. Three months later, he was diagnosed with stage-four lung cancer. Though the oncologist had initially given him six months to live, he'd only made it four.

That was almost three years ago. Now my mother was next in line to meet the Reaper.

"I hope if there's a Hell, you burn in it." Not that she and my father had practiced religion. They'd dragged us to church on Easter and Christmas, but otherwise, the only time we ever heard about the Good Book was during an occasional history class at school.

Regardless, the idea of my mother burning in a lake of fire for all eternity tempered a bit of my lingering irritation. I snatched the top photo—I'd printed more than twenty—and made my way out to the range.

Even though my brother and I were the only ones with the code to get into this room, I always took down the photos I used for target practice before I left. In fact, I made sure nothing in here could be tied back to our hunts. Not even the crossbows. We had separate storage for the items we used in hunts.

As I pinned my mother's photo in position, I offered her a smile. "I'm sure you'd just *love* the updates I've made to this place." I gestured at the wires crisscrossing above my head. "I fixed it up so I could practice on moving targets. Though, honestly, I wish I could figure out a way to do some real practice."

Practice all you want, but you'll never be good enough.

I could almost hear her voice.

Turning back toward the counter, I gritted my teeth. "I know, I know. None of this is appropriate for a woman of my social status. Let's not forget you were the one who insisted we go to that stupid camp in the first place. I can only assume it's because you didn't want to deal with us over the summer, so you figured out a way to get rid of us."

I let out a dry laugh. We were eleven when my parents shipped us off to summer camp. Never mind that we'd never stepped foot in the wilderness, that we'd spent our entire lives in the heart of Chicago.

Popping the lid off the plastic container, I scooped up a handful of bolts and arranged them neatly beside my bow. I raised a shoulder and peered out at the distant photo.

"Don't worry, Mother. I'm sure your eldest son...your favorite son...will be here soon. I'm not quite sure why you asked me to take care of you on your deathbed instead of Eddie. Then again, maybe you did, and he refused. Could it be that all your offspring despise you?"

I hadn't already finished my mother off only because she'd had the foresight to offer me a substantial chunk of the inheritance...with a string attached, of course. I had to visit her daily with my daughter in tow.

The one time I'd forgotten the little brat, my mother hadn't shut up about it for the duration of the visit, waffling between berating me and reconciling. I was sure the woman had lost her marbles.

And while I knew the notion was absurd, part of me wondered if one or more of the nurses tending to the woman were actually paralegals in disguise working for her dipshit lawyer. I couldn't take the chance of losing the money I was due.

Her proposal had taken me aback at first, but the more I thought about it, the more sense it made. My mother didn't want me to visit her. She wanted my daughter to keep her company in her final days.

Or she was attempting to buy my love after a lifetime of neglect. The few words she offered did nothing to repair the damage she'd already done.

"This better not last much longer, Mother. Your time is up. I don't see the point of clinging to your final few days."

I clenched my jaw and shook my head, as if the motion would erase the stress eating away at my sanity.

It wouldn't, though. Nothing aside from a good hunt would chase away this niggling in the back of my mind. Out there in the wilderness, hot on the trail of some scared nitwit, I was free. I could be my true self without judgment and ridicule.

Out there, I had *real* power.

My brother and I used to go on hunts once or twice a year. Now we'd already been on two this month. I wasn't sure how wise it was for us to revisit Lake Henrietta after we'd hunted there a few years ago, but with Mother creeping closer to death's door each day, we couldn't stray as far as we used to.

It didn't matter. We were thorough. *They'll never find my errant crossbow bolt. It went into the river—it's probably been washed into the Mississippi by now. I pulled the bolts from the other bodies, so they'll have nothing.*

Just like they used to teach us at that summer camp. *Leave no trace.*

Who knew lessons about saving the environment would translate so well into the activities of my adult life?

We worked together to hoist the bodies and fling them out into the river. The current was strong enough to pull them into the lake, which was only a hop, skip, and a jump away. No witnesses. And once the water had washed them clean, no trace evidence.

I raised my crossbow, tightening the stock against my shoulder as I peered down the sights.

It was possible the cops would find the bodies, though. They'd uncovered our victims before—not that it mattered. If I was honest with myself, I rather enjoyed watching those plebians chase their tails as they searched for clues. My brother and I had perfected our craft over the years, so no backwoods Rosco P. Coltrane sheriff was going to outsmart us.

How many people out there knew about us without even realizing who we were?

The idea brought goose bumps to my forearms.

My first shot ripped through my mother's forehead, and the second took out her nose. That stupid button nose she'd always compared to mine.

"You should consider rhinoplasty. I can schedule an appointment for your sixteenth birthday, you know."

I ground my teeth together. Another imperfection my mother liked to point out.

"If you keep doing that, your smile will never attract a suitable husband. Unless, of course, you want dentures at twenty."

Critiquing my appearance was the only reason that bitch ever bothered to speak to me. Otherwise, she'd hardly acknowledged my existence.

"Well, Mother, that cute little button nose and those pearly whites won't do you a lot of good when your corpse is food for the worms. Maybe if you'd done a better job of taking care of yourself, you wouldn't be biting the dust at your age."

Satisfied with the practice shots on a stationary target, I grabbed two more photos of my mother and hung them in place. As I switched on the overhead machinery that would move each target in a zigzag pattern, I turned my entire focus on hitting that woman's stupid nose again.

I repeated the process a couple of times, and after each hit, I stacked up the spent pictures so I could show Garrett the next time he teased me about missing that pathetic kid at Lake Henrietta.

I could've stayed in my range for the rest of the night,

blissfully unaware of any other goings-on in this house. But a knock at the door ripped my attention away from the newest, partially punctured photo of my mother.

Fighting a desire to scream and tell them to piss off, I set down the crossbow and curled my hands into tight fists.

If this is one of the housekeepers, they're fired. They should know better than to interrupt me.

"Mom? Are you in there?"

"What do you want?" I didn't bother to conceal my annoyance. "I'm busy right now."

The brat was fourteen, so there was no sense in coddling her. Not that my idiot husband agreed, but I didn't care about his opinion. I was in charge, not him. Just because my father gave him a position on our company's board of directors didn't mean he got to call the shots in my house.

When my daughter didn't immediately respond, I turned toward the door.

The little shit didn't get to supersede my authority, either, but there wasn't much I could do. Not until she turned eighteen and I could kick her ass to the curb.

"I...um...I need you to approve something for school. So I can go on a field trip the last week in May."

I rolled my eyes. "Can't you ask your father? I'm busy right now."

"N-no. He's...he's not home."

Ugh. The stammer in her voice made me want to open the door and slap her across the face.

Grow a backbone, kid. When I was your age...

I scrubbed a hand over my face. I'd wanted my daughter to grow up tough, mentally and physically, but my husband had turned her into a powder puff.

One thing at a time. I was already having to spend time with the kid when I dragged her to the mandatory visits of old Mommy Dearest. Why didn't she ask me then? This spawn needed to learn a lesson, but that would have to wait until my mother was six feet under.

Clenching and unclenching my hands, I took a deep breath. "All right. I'll be out in a few minutes."

"Okay. Thank you."

Another meek response.

Was there any hope for her?

I rolled my head to release the knots forming in my neck. All this pretending had begun to wear on me, and there was only so much satisfaction I could get from firing crossbow bolts at photos of my mother. Maybe I'd hang up my daughter's school pictures next target practice.

Maybe. But these flimsy stand-ins could only keep me satiated for so long.

Pretty soon, I'd need the real thing again.

13

Keeping an eye on the gathering storm clouds, Amelia and Dean left Lake Henrietta in the care of the crime scene techs—the fewer people sloshing through the muddy ground, the less likely someone would inadvertently ruin a potential piece of evidence. Too many cooks in the kitchen, as the old saying went.

Since they were both a sticky, dirty mess, they swung by their B and B for quick showers and clean clothes. Fresh and renewed, Amelia snatched a sandwich from the platter their host had set out for them. Though her feet were sore from all the hiking she'd done already, she texted Dean that she would walk the short distance to the sheriff's office. The shower had given her a second wind.

Donning a rain jacket at the front door, she mentally congratulated herself for packing exactly what she needed, no matter what anyone said.

At the station, she flashed her badge at the deputy who managed the reception desk of the Jordan County Sheriff's Office. The young man responded with a nod and a polite smile before showing her where to hang up her jacket and directing her to their makeshift incident room. The space was typically reserved for small meetings, but despite its postage-stamp size, it contained a table, chairs, and a whiteboard. Since it included a steady internet connection, Amelia couldn't ask for much more from their gracious hosts.

Flicking on the overhead lights, she slung her messenger bag onto the table and got to work unpacking her laptop as well as the camera she'd carried during her trek around Lake Henrietta.

Though the CSU would have their own photographs, as far as Amelia was concerned, there was no such thing as too many pictures of a crime scene. She'd already uploaded them into the official case file, ensuring she adhered to chain of custody. Now she could take her time studying each one.

Her cell buzzed against the table before she could power on her laptop. Scooping up the phone, her spirits lightened as she spotted Zane's name on the screen.

With a smile tugging at her mouth, she tapped the green answer icon and leaned back in her chair. "Hey, how's life treating you in the big city?"

"In the big city? Are you already adopting the small-town nomenclature?" His light, jovial tone was a welcome change from the grim air that'd followed Amelia for much of the afternoon.

"Oh, no. Not even close. I could never live without my twenty-four-hour pizza joints and Thai restaurants every two blocks. You know I need plenty of dining options to survive." Having been born and raised in Chicago, Amelia doubted she'd last a week in a small town like Henrietta City.

"That's true, I suppose. I doubt there're many places to

get chicken tikka masala and samosas in a county with the same population as a single block in Chicago." Zane was exaggerating, but not by much.

At the mention of one of her favorite Indian dishes, Amelia suddenly found the chicken salad croissant in her hand unsatisfying. "No, there aren't. But the bed-and-breakfast we're staying at has excellent taste in coffee. The owner is so nice too. As soon as Steelman and I got back from working in the field, she brewed us a fresh pot and set out some homemade sandwiches and cookies."

"Okay, well, if you've got a ready supply of fresh-baked cookies, you can probably survive a few days. How's work going? Did you guys find anything out at Lake Henrietta? I looked that place up earlier, and it seems...nice, I guess. A couple hikers went missing a few years ago, and apparently, a couple from Chicago went there for a camping trip and never came back home."

Curiosity piqued, Amelia straightened in her chair and turned on her laptop. "What did you find? Show me yours and I'll show you mine."

He chuckled. "Any day. Any time."

She missed him already. "Hold that thought, mister. Let's compare notes right now."

"Nothing earth-shattering, and this all might be in your file already, but in case it isn't..." Keys clicked in the background. "There were some articles that mentioned people going missing in the area. I had to sift through a few pages of search results."

Amelia pulled up a search engine. "That far back?"

"Since there were no bodies found, I'm guessing it didn't exactly make front-page news. The few articles I found speculated that the missing people might've drowned in the lake or one of the rivers nearby. I was mostly curious to see if

Lake Henrietta was known for being a place where killers dumped bodies in the past."

News headlines never ceased to amaze Amelia. There were plenty of good reporters out there, but unfortunately, they were often overshadowed by more sensational headlines—news about celebrities and politicians, mainly.

Zack Hartman of the *National Horizon* was one of the good ones. He'd run a story that helped Amelia and Zane with a case involving a sitting U.S. Senator.

"We've been out in the field until just a little bit ago, so I haven't had time to do much research on the area yet. It sounds like you might've just saved me some time. We'll take a look at those missing people and send their info over to the Cook County M.E. so they can do some comparisons."

"Seems like a good start. What did you guys find at Lake Henrietta? Anything promising?"

"Yeah, a few things. But we had to get through it all quickly, since a storm blew in."

As Amelia filled Zane in on her quick tutorial on tracking and the details uncovered by Deputy Foveaux's expert eye—including the scene where the two most recent victims appeared to have been murdered—the entire conversation came naturally. For a beat, she almost forgot Zane wasn't her case partner.

After an update on Hup—namely, how she hadn't moved more than five feet away from Zane since he'd gotten home—they said their goodbyes. Amelia was about to start a new online search for news about Lake Henrietta when the door swung open to reveal none other than...a very sleepy looking Dean.

Pausing in the doorway, her partner blinked a few times before stepping inside and glancing at his watch. "Am I...

late? I feel like I'm late. Didn't we say we'd meet back here at eight? I swear I just closed my eyes for a minute and—"

"Huh? No, no, you're not late." Amelia sized up his plaid shirt. "But if you need more time to go back and change into a clean shirt, go ahead."

He looked down. Confusion etched into his features before a smile spread across his face. "We can't all overpack, Storm. You'd think after your time in the military you'd have learned to be more efficient." He patted his chest and mocked wiping dust off his shoulder. "Take note for the next time we're shipped off somewhere. I smell just fine, by the way."

She held in a chortle. "I like to think I'm prepared for anything. Anyway, you're not late. I just wanted to get a head start on researching Lake Henrietta. Well, technically Zane did the research earlier today, and I'm just following what he did, but you know..." She shrugged.

"Oh, so Palmer's with us in spirit, then?" Unshouldering his laptop bag, Dean dropped down to sit across from her. "Good. I'm glad to hear it. What did you find?"

"Nothing yet. I was just about to start my search." While Dean unloaded his bag and set up his laptop, Amelia gave him a rundown of what Zane had shared with her, minus the details about Hup.

"Two pairs of folks going missing from Lake Henrietta in the past three years. That lines up with the states of decomp Dr. Islas reported." Dean's fingers tapped along his keyboard with dexterity and speed that still surprised Amelia. The man had to type at least a hundred words per minute.

"They're on their way to Cook County now. Should be there in the next few hours. Divers will resume their search tomorrow, but the CSU is still working the site by the river... or at least, they said they'd work until sunset."

He glanced out the window. "I'd say they'll work until the storm hits."

"We've got plenty of ground to cover ourselves." Amelia began to count off tasks on her fingers. "There's the search for missing persons around Lake Henrietta. Then a deep dive into Jeremy Fitzgerald's and Leslie Armstrong's backgrounds and following up on whatever's there. We need to look into the campgrounds. And lastly, for now, anyway, we need to run the details of these murders through ViCAP."

The Violent Criminal Apprehension Program, a database maintained by the FBI and utilized by law enforcement across the country, was designed to track and correlate information about violent crimes, especially those that might indicate serial offenses, such as murders and sexual assaults. Any homicides that appeared random or crimes that exhibited a distinct "signature" suggestive of a serial offender were entered into the database, where they could later be compared with future similar crimes and potentially help identify patterns or link serial crimes.

Dean rubbed his chin. "We should fill in a few of the blanks, then go through Leslie's and Jeremy's backgrounds to figure out where they fit in all this. What do you think?"

Amelia was glad they were operating on the same wavelength. "Sure. Fill in the blanks we can with a little research, so we have a better idea of the scope we're dealing with. I'll take ViCAP if you want to research Lake Henrietta?"

He shot her a thumbs-up. "Sounds like a plan."

Amelia and Dean tapped away at their keyboards. The *click-clack* of plastic keys and the patter of raindrops against the window were the only sounds in the small room.

He paused to roll up his sleeves. "The campground's been around since the seventies. It started by offering only non-electric sites for tent campers. Over the years, it looks like they've added a few electric hookups. There's also space for RVs, though that's more limited. It won an award in the late nineties for its amenities, but otherwise, it isn't terribly remarkable."

"Okay, well, I guess we couldn't expect a Yelp review stating it was a great place to dump bodies."

Dean chuckled.

Amelia finished entering the final details of Leslie's and Jeremy's murders into ViCAP and started the search.

The laptop's fan hummed quietly as the results populated.

"Shit..." The expletive slipped from Amelia's lips unbidden.

Dean's head jerked up from his laptop, his gaze locking onto hers. "What? Is that a bad *shit* or a good *shit*?"

Blowing out a lengthy breath, Amelia leaned back in her chair. "Bad. Definitely bad. I entered in as many of the unique details as I could, but I don't think I needed them. The symbol carved on the victims' skulls is distinctive enough."

One of Dean's eyebrows quirked up. "I take it there're others?"

Amelia scrolled to the bottom of the search results, her stomach sinking with each one. "There are a lot of others, all with that specific rune carved into their skulls. They go back almost ten years."

"Ten years." He crossed both arms over his plaid shirt, his chair creaking with the movement. "Huh. Well, it sounds like we've only just scratched the surface."

14

Amelia had emptied her coffee an hour ago, yet her head brimmed with names, dates, and locations. Though many of the crimes had occurred in the Midwest, there were linked murders reported as far west as California and as far south as Louisiana. With eighteen sets of victims—including those uncovered at Lake Henrietta—the investigation had quickly grown in scope.

They'd reached out to each of the jurisdictions, requesting the case files and letting them know they had linked cases. As Amelia had scrawled information on the whiteboard, even Dean, a seasoned veteran of the Bureau's Violent Crime Unit, began muttering surprised exclamations under his breath.

Returning the marker to a mug on top of a file cabinet in the corner of the room, Amelia stepped back to observe the board. "So if we count Jeremy Fitzgerald, Leslie Armstrong, and Jane Does One and Two, we're looking at thirty-six victims."

Dean rose to stand, stretching both arms above his head. "There's a clear pattern across these cases. Two vics each cycle, usually one male and one female, but not always. The consistent aspects are that there are always *two* victims and they all have the rune carved into their skulls. So far, we've got Jeremy and Leslie, who were obviously together. According to the preliminary report Dr. Islas filed before she left for Chicago, the other two vics were killed years apart. Jane Doe One has been dead for weeks, but Jane Doe Two has been at the bottom of Lake Henrietta for years."

Amelia caught onto the implication of his statement. "You think there are more bodies in that lake?"

With a nod, Dean meandered toward the window. "I'd put money on it. It's a private place, it's obviously worked for our perpetrator or perpetrators before, and there are still some missing persons locally who've never been located. There are *four* people who've gone missing from this area over the last three years. Kayla and Otto Hampton, who were last seen two and a half weeks ago, and Angie Marsh and Ron Dawson, who've been missing for almost three years."

Amelia suppressed the urge to mimic his pacing. The postage-stamp room could accommodate only so much movement. "Okay, so since our vics are both female, we're thinking Otto and Ron are both still at the bottom of Lake Henrietta."

He turned, covering the length of the room yet again. "I wouldn't rule out the possibility that the current carried them to the Mississippi and we may never recover either one of them. But until the M.E.'s office makes a positive ID, hunches are about all we've got. I checked all their records, and they haven't had any kind of activity since they were reported missing. No financial activity whatsoever. So far, none of them have been found. I think it's safe to assume, based on the patterns we're seeing, that Ron and Otto are dead too."

The abrupt disappearances were a strong argument in favor of Dean's theory. Plus, he was right. For the time being, patterns were their best source of information.

"First, we're working under the assumption from Foveaux's findings at the lake that we're dealing with two killers, correct?"

Dean finally paused his pacing to gaze at the board. "It certainly seems that way, yeah."

"All right." Amelia gestured at the list of names. "Since the case here in Jordan County is still developing, let's look at the next most recent murder outside the county. Seven months ago, end of September. Two victims, identified as Brant and Amanda Lowery, both found in Signet Lake just south of Parkdale, Minnesota. Estimated time of death was mid-September."

"Middle of September, then dormant again until mid-April." Dean scratched his chin, his gaze fixed on the whiteboard. "They're targeting campers, so the period of dormancy could be the months when people don't really go camping."

Pulling out her chair, Amelia returned to her seat and reached for her laptop. There was so much information to comb through, she had to ensure she stayed organized. "I pulled case notes for each incident. The Lowery case was taken over by the FBI in Duluth once the locals realized they were dealing with a serial killer. According to the case notes, the rune carved in the victims' skulls is Norse. It roughly translates to *Fe*, or *Fehu*, which can mean wealth or money, or even cattle or sheep."

Dean's eyebrows knitted together. "Cattle? So is this them branding their victims like they own them?" He let out a derisive snort. "Christ, these fucking perps are something else."

Amelia agreed with Dean's less-than-favorable view of the killers. Not only were they deranged, but if the reasoning behind the Fehu rune was to label victims as cattle, then these psychopaths had some sort of god complex.

"The case notes for Signet Lake also indicate there were two killers, which is consistent with what we have here. One set of footprints found at the scene was a men's size twelve, approximately, and the other was a men's size eight."

"Fits with the size of the tracks we found. We'll have to get in touch with the Duluth office tomorrow. I'm sure they'll be more than happy to hand this over to us. Is that the only case out of Minnesota?"

"No, there was one other. Alexandria, Minnesota, bodies found in Lake Reno. Identified as Bobby and Dale Hodge. They were killed almost two years ago, in July. Technically, the Duluth office was investigating both sets of murders, but the cases went cold." The more Amelia learned about the previous cases, the bleaker the situation became.

Through ViCAP, the Minnesota agents had also linked their four victims to the twenty-eight others. Despite the litany of old cases and clues, they'd come no closer to solving the crimes than those before them.

Stifling a yawn, Dean moved back to his chair. "The interval between murders is getting shorter."

"The cooling off period. The time they can go until they're compelled to kill again." Pressing her lips together, Amelia turned to the dry-erase board. "You're right. They've gone from ten months between the first two, to six or seven months consistently. Until now. There were only two weeks between the two most recent sets of murders." The first tendrils of unease wound their way into Amelia's gut.

Dean flattened his hands against the table. "My guess? Some sort of external stressor. We can run this by the BAU, but I bet that's what they'll say. A lot of the time, serials will cope with stressful life events by escalating. And usually, there's no putting that genie back in the bottle once it's out."

"Yeah." Amelia thought back to everything she knew about serial killers. "Meaning they'll likely keep killing at shorter and shorter intervals, even after their stressor is gone."

"Not always, but we ought to be prepared for the worst." Leaning back, he stifled another yawn. "Sorry. It's been a long day."

As much as Amelia wanted to keep researching until she dropped from exhaustion, her case partner's yawn was contagious.

We won't do this investigation any good if our exhaustion leads us to miss something important.

The stakes were too high for that.

Numerous law enforcement agencies had struggled to find leads before now, and as a result, these two killers had racked up a body count approaching forty.

But eventually, every killer made a mistake. After a decade, they had to slip up.

Matter of time.

Amelia would leave no stone unturned. One way or another, she'd find their Achilles' heel and use it to bring them down once and for all.

15

Because of his time in the military, Dean was a light sleeper. The comfort of his own home helped the borderline insomnia, but when he was traveling, even the slightest disturbances woke him. It was a blessing and a curse, but lately, mostly a curse.

He was about to ask his fishing partner, Sandra Bullock, to pass him a lure, when the familiar chime of his phone's ringtone cut through their sunny afternoon. For a beat, he and the actress were both confused, but reality didn't take long to rip Dean away from the bizarre yet idyllic scene.

Snapping his eyes open wide, he was greeted with... darkness. Shadows coalesced in the corners of his room, the entire scene a far cry from his dream world. As he blinked to clear his vision, he pushed himself into a sitting position. The details of his strange dream faded, only to be replaced by reality.

You're not at Tina's B and B because you're on a fishing trip with a movie star. You're here because you're investigating four—no, scratch that—thirty-six murders. And your phone's ringing. Rise and shine, shithead.

As his cell started to buzz against the nightstand for the second or third time, Dean grabbed the device. He didn't recognize the number, but he noted the area code was local to Jordan County.

Clearing his throat, he swiped the screen to answer the call. "This is Agent Steelman."

"Good morning, Agent Steelman. This is Patsy Wilkerson with the crime scene unit. I hope I didn't wake you. I assumed you'd be in the incident room."

Dean's mind summoned up the likeness of the tenured crime scene tech who'd processed much of Jeremy Fitzgerald and Leslie Armstrong's campsite. Noting the time on his phone, he silently cursed his erratic sleep patterns. "I won't bore you with the reasons why I'm not there yet. What can I help you with?"

"We've got something."

A rush of anticipation flooded Dean's veins, his fatigue all but forgotten. "What'd you find?"

"A crossbow bolt, believe it or not. It was embedded in the trunk of a tree on the other side of the river. We're getting it bagged and tagged, but I thought you and Agent Storm might want to see it in person."

Hell, yes, we would.

Tossing the covers off, he got to his feet in an instant. "Of course. Let me grab Agent Storm, and we'll head out to the site."

"All right. We'll see you soon."

Dean called Amelia's cell. She was downstairs enjoying their B and B hostess's homemade muffins and locally roasted coffee. Even though her mouth was full of food, an unmistakable twinge of excitement underscored her voice when he told her the news. After hanging up, he dressed, brushed his teeth, and hurried down to the lobby where

Amelia was waiting for him, her dark hair pulled back into a ponytail and a cross-body handbag slung over her shoulder.

To Dean's delight, she held up two travel mugs full of coffee. "I asked Tina if she'd brew us enough to take along."

"No complaint here. Mrs. Barker has been a great hostess." Grateful for her foresight, Dean accepted one of the travel mugs and cracked it open. The beverage tasted like battery acid so soon after brushing his teeth, but the caffeinated infusion worked to chase away the lingering strands of sleep from his brain.

As they made their way to their black SUV, Dean was relieved to note the orange and pink hues painting the horizon. The glow of the sun was strong enough to keep them from stumbling blindly through the unfamiliar muddy woodland around Lake Henrietta.

Neither of them spoke much on the short trip while they polished off their drinks. At the site, the sun's golden rays pierced the sky, now a dusty blue, as they stepped out of the vehicle. Dean had only just closed the driver's side door when his attention snapped to a familiar man trotting toward them and waving.

"Deputy Hester." Dean returned the young man's wave. "I take it you're here to lead us to the discovery?"

"That's right." Hester grinned. "Patsy and I just got back on duty about an hour ago, and we've got the divers coming in about," he glanced at his watch, "an hour and a half. Everyone got your messages about those folks who went missing a couple weeks ago and the other two who disappeared three years ago. Once the sun's finished coming up, we'll resume the search to look for signs of another abandoned campsite."

Dean was grateful for the aid of the sheriff's department. Chasing thirty-six murders was a massive burden for two

FBI agents, but Hester's update reassured him that he and Amelia had plenty of good people on their team. "That's great. We appreciate how coordinated you guys have been."

The young deputy's expression brightened even more. "We're here to help. And, speaking of, let's head over to the river."

Though the trek started out smoothly enough, the dripping leaves from the thickening canopy overhead soon blocked out the illumination of the sun. Their three flashlights bobbed as they trudged along the muddy earth, Dean nearly losing his balance on two separate occasions. The incline leading to the riverbank was only slight, but with the ground so mushy and soaked, he had to watch his step.

As Dean and Amelia emerged in the clearing, only about half the personnel from the previous evening were present. The CSU had arrived at sunrise to continue processing the scene and save any remaining evidence. They'd then determined there wasn't much left to salvage and told the rest of their team not to come.

Patsy Wilkerson beckoned the agents over to where she and a younger man stood near a steep drop-off to the river below. "Good morning. I'm glad you could make it here so quickly." She gestured to the skinny guy at her side. "This is Phil Carlson, another member of the CSU for Jordan County. He's our ballistics expert, and he specializes in physics and mathematics so the rest of us don't have to."

Patsy's early morning humor reminded Dean of his usual case partner. Right then, he was almost glad Sherry wasn't here. He couldn't imagine what her and Patsy's banter would be like at the ass crack of dawn.

Once Amelia and Dean had made their introductions to Carlson, Patsy bade them farewell and headed toward another pair of crime scene techs near the tree line. A long plastic table had been set up along with a tarp to keep it dry, serving as a makeshift evidence-processing station.

Flipping open the case of a sleek tablet, Phil cradled the device in one arm as he produced a laser pointer from his jacket. "Well, you got here at a good time. We're finished with the tedious work, and we've got plenty of photographs and video to show you. But first, here's the location of the bolt." He clicked on the pointer, shining the powerful beam on a small tree on the opposite bank of the river.

In place of the crossbow bolt, the CSU had inserted a clear plastic rod that faintly glowed green. Having examined his fair share of crime scenes, Dean recognized the arrangement right away. "You got a laser set up to calculate the trajectory?"

"Yep, sure did. Lucky for us, it was still dark at the time, so we got plenty of good shots of the laser. Mother Nature even helped us out with a little fog from that storm." After turning off the pointer, Phil powered on the tablet. "With the sun coming up, I think it'd be easier to show you the video and photos we took than it would be to do an actual demonstration. Here, take a look."

Tapping the screen, Phil passed the tablet to Dean. As Amelia scooted closer, a sliver of green light glowed to life on the right side of the screen. Though the scene was much darker, Dean made out the shape of the tree and the plastic rod stuck into the trunk.

As a shroud of fog rolled over the already misty scene, the beam of the laser stood out in stark contrast.

Amelia studied the area around them. "So according to the trajectory of the laser, it looks like the shooter was standing on this side of the river, right?"

Phil nodded. "Right. Check out the next video."

Dean swiped the screen, revealing a view quite similar to

where he and Amelia stood. Once again, thick fog poured into the shot, illuminating the green laser.

"We took plenty of stills too. Got all that done before the sun started to rise." Phil gestured to the tablet. "Now, by using those photos, I pinpointed the most likely position for the shooter. The area of probability. It's right over here, about halfway between the tree line and the edge of the riverbank. There's a stretch of ground where the shooter could've been standing, depending on their height."

As Dean followed Phil's outstretched hand, his cautious optimism sank. What had been a patch of dirt before the storm was now a muddy, soupy mess. "Well, that doesn't look promising."

The ballistics expert was unfazed. "There's not much we can get from it now, but we've taken plenty of photos. We'll compare them to the photos we took yesterday of that same area to see if the shooter left any prints behind."

Of course. Dean and Amelia had both taken close to a million pictures the day before, and they also had the documentation from the crime scene unit.

Cautious optimism replaced Dean's moment of pessimism. "We can do that, yeah. Is there anything else you can tell us about the projectile?"

"It was clean. No blood or tissue, so I don't think it hit anything or anyone." Phil tapped his cheek. "I haven't worked a ton of cases involving crossbow bolts, but this isn't the first. The bolts usually travel at around three hundred feet per second, whereas a handgun bullet often exceeds a thousand, long guns even more. The slower speed is obvious from the angle of the bolt. If it had moved faster, it would've been embedded in the tree at a more acute angle. The slower the projectile travels, the quicker it loses altitude."

Having always excelled at trigonometry and physics, Dean understood the fundamentals of Phil's explanation. With a quick farewell and the reassurance that Dean would return his tablet when he and Amelia were finished scouting the scene, Phil set off for the evidence station, leaving the agents in the approximate location where a crossbow-wielding serial killer had once stood.

Amelia pulled a tablet from her handbag. "Let's compare the images side by side."

Dean pointed at a sapling sprouting between two larger maples. "That little tree is a good indication of where we should be looking. In the video, the laser cut right past it." He flipped through a few images to find a still of the scene, holding out the screen for Amelia.

Nodding her understanding, she turned back to the tablet. After a few moments of searching in silence, she snapped her fingers. "Here we go. A whole series of pictures I took of that exact area. And...the reason I took so many was because we found footprints there. A few of them, all made by the same person."

A jolt of excitement ran up Dean's spine, and he peered down at the screen in Amelia's hands. Sure enough, she scrolled through more than a dozen images of the dirt in front of the sapling. In one of the last photos, a pair of faint shoe impressions were visible through the thin grass. Amelia zoomed in on the spot, then pointed at the ground six feet away from the sapling.

For a better comparison, Dean held Phil's tablet next to hers. "You can see the laser shining right above that same spot, the same distance in front of the little tree. How far off the ground do you think that is?"

Amelia's eyebrows scrunched together. "I'm not sure. Five feet, maybe? We can get a more accurate measurement if we use the tree as a ruler. But I can tell you the footprints in that area were made from the smaller of the two perps."

"All right. Let's measure that tree and give all this info to Phil. While I'm capable of doing the calculation, I'd feel better leaving it in the hands of an expert."

Amelia's face brightened with an amused smile. "Oh, I agree completely. I don't mind noodling over a good math problem, but I haven't needed to do much trigonometry lately."

Returning her grin, Dean started toward the evidence table. Though the discovery of the crossbow wielder's footprints was satisfying, he and Amelia still had a mountain of work before they could fit the knowledge into any useful context.

For the moment, he permitted himself a sense of accomplishment. Without the small wins, cases tended to spin out of control. A frustrated investigator was an investigator who made mistakes, and with thirty-six victims that they knew of, they couldn't afford a single mishap.

16

Amelia had been awake since just after sunrise, but despite her lack of sleep, she was full of energy and focus. An early lunch from one of the local bars, while not nutritious, helped fuel her before she and Dean prepared to meet with a potential witness. As Amelia stepped out into the abundant sunshine, she blinked repeatedly and reached for her sunglasses.

With the sun climbing into a clear blue sky and a temperature hovering in the low seventies, she could imagine why so many locals were drawn to Lake Henrietta. In a town of only three thousand people, what else was there to do in their free time? Then again, the solitude and scenery were likely the very reasons the residents lived there.

As Dean emerged through the open door—held in place by Amelia, a gesture which had earned her the title of "a true gentleman" from Zane—the two of them headed to the SUV. The black vehicle and its darkly tinted windows were sorely out of place in a lot filled with white sheriff's cars.

Amelia climbed into the passenger seat, fastening her

seat belt as Dean brought the engine to life. Fortunately, the witness they sought lived only fifteen minutes outside town.

Earlier in the day, having notified next of kin the night before, the sheriff's department had aired a radio and television broadcast to ask for any locals who'd been at or near Lake Henrietta on the night Jeremy Fitzgerald and Leslie Armstrong were killed to come forward. The announcement included their driver's license photos in the hopes that someone might recall seeing one or both victims.

The case was still unfolding, so the department hadn't given any specific details of the crimes. Just that they were investigating a double homicide at the Lake Henrietta Wilderness Preserve, as well as another homicide that had occurred two weeks prior. Since the fourth body found was only a few bones and had likely been killed years prior, that victim was left out of the announcement. The theory was that it was too long ago for anyone's memory to be fresh.

Amelia could hardly imagine being the citizen of a small, quiet town—believing she was safe from the violence of larger cities, from the turmoil that plagued so much of the country—only to awaken one morning and find that evil had showed up on her doorstep.

Learning that nowhere was safe from such tragedies was a hard pill to swallow, and the town's growing unease created a shroud everywhere they traveled.

When the citizens of Henrietta City went to bed that night, many of them would lock their doors for the first time in years, maybe even decades. They'd keep a closer watch on their neighbors, and the gossip train would leave the station in a rush. Then, when they found out the victims were murdered by a serial killer...

"This is why we can't have nice things."

Zane's voice was clear as day in Amelia's head. Though

he used the saying often, he'd made the observation more than once as they investigated yet another brutal murder.

Stretching her arms, Amelia worked kinks from her muscles she never knew she could feel from trekking around in the woods. "Steelman, did you grow up in a small town?"

If the query caught Dean off guard, he gave no indication. "Sure did."

"In West Virginia?"

"Yep. Lived there 'til I turned eighteen and joined the military."

"How do you think the people there would've reacted to four dead bodies showing up out of the blue one day?"

To Amelia's surprise, Dean barked out a laugh. "They made lots of meth around where I grew up, so no one would've blinked. It was a small town, sure, but it wasn't a *nice* small town. There's a reason I got the hell out of there the second I could."

Despite the grim subject matter, Amelia joined in his laughter. "Fair enough. What'd you think about that crossbow bolt? Have you ever handled a weapon like that?"

"Nah. Hunting was never really my scene. I like fishing, but I'm more of a catch-and-release guy. And no way can I hunt deer. Have you seen a deer in person? They're cute. Those eyes. Not that I've got any problems with hunting. Some places rely on deer hunters to thin out the population to keep the ecosystem in check. I'm just not the guy to do it. I like animals too much."

His response was both expected and surprising. The more Amelia learned about Dean Steelman, the more she realized he didn't fit neatly into any one box.

Maybe that's why we get along so well.

For the rest of the short trip, they discussed the potential witness they were about to visit. Tommy Mercer was as clean-cut as any man in his late forties could possibly be. He'd lived in Jordan County all his life, and he was beloved by the entire Henrietta City community. When his wife passed away from breast cancer two years earlier, the town had rallied around Tommy to raise more than fifty thousand dollars to pay down his medical debt.

At the end of a short gravel drive, Dean pulled the SUV to a stop in a gently sloping driveway that led to a two-car garage. Before Amelia had even unfastened her seat belt, the front door of the house swung open to reveal a man dressed quite similarly to her partner—dark jeans and a red-and-white plaid shirt, minus the jacket Dean wore to conceal his service weapon.

With his salt-and-pepper hair pulled back into a ponytail and the same neatly kempt beard he'd sported in his driver's license photo, Amelia recognized Tommy Mercer right away.

The middle-aged man pushed open the screen door and stepped into the shade of the covered porch. "Hello, there. You must be the federal agents who're in town to help with those bodies they found over in Lake Henrietta?" His words were as much a question as a statement.

As Dean circled around to the sidewalk, Amelia produced her badge. "Yes, sir. We spoke on the phone a little bit ago. I'm Special Agent Amelia Storm, and this is my case partner, Special Agent Dean Steelman."

With a polite nod, Dean flashed his credentials.

"Nice to meet you. I'm Tommy. You wanted to talk about Lake Henrietta, right? About when I was out there camping a few nights ago?" He held open the door as Amelia and Dean climbed the few steps to the porch. "Come on in. I just brewed a pot of coffee when I got your call. Figured with everything going on, you could probably use a little boost."

Even if Amelia hadn't read up on Tommy's background before meeting him, his genuine smile and warm demeanor made her like him right away. The frequent locations of the killers implied they either traveled for their job or had means, but Tommy Mercer was as blue-collar as they came. His job at the local tackle shop would've kept him mired here in town, especially during the months typically considered to be hunting season.

With these details in mind, Amelia doubted he'd committed all the murders across the country over the past decade. Still, serial killers were known to insinuate themselves into cases, so she wouldn't let her guard down just yet.

After leading Amelia and Dean to a cozy living room with a sectional couch, a recliner, and a massive, wall-mounted television, Tommy made his way around the corner to the kitchen. Moments later, he emerged with three steaming cups of coffee.

"As promised." He offered them a smile as he placed a mug on the small wooden table in front of Amelia and Dean. Settling into his recliner, Tommy blew on his coffee, his expression curious.

"Much appreciated, Mr. Mercer." Amelia held up her coffee and returned the smile. "We'll try to make this quick so you can get on with your day."

He lifted a shoulder. "Call me Tommy. No rush. I'm off work for the rest of the week. I kicked off my vacation time with a little camping out by Lake Henrietta." His face fell. "Which is why you're here to talk to me. Those poor kids. What can I do to help?"

After sipping his own coffee, Dean replaced the mug on the table and produced a notebook and pen from within his canvas jacket. "We're hoping you can tell us about your camping trip on Saturday."

Appearing to focus, the man straightened in his seat. "Okay. Sure. I took my RV and my boat out to Lake Henrietta to do some hiking and photography. My wife, Erin...she always loved taking pictures, so it's just something I sorta picked up after she passed. Makes me feel a little closer to her even though she's gone, you know?"

The story tugged at Amelia's heart strings, but it also piqued her curiosity. "Photography? Do you still have the pictures you took?"

Tommy sipped his coffee. "I do, yeah. Haven't quite gotten around to going through them, so they ought to all still be there. Why? Do you think I might've gotten something?"

"It's possible." Amelia kept her sudden excitement in check, her tone calm and reassuring. She pulled a business card from her wallet and set it on the coffee table. "We'll leave you our cards, if you could email us all the photos you took..."

"I'll do you one better. Before you leave, I'll load all the photos onto a memory card you can take with you. I've got tons of those cards lying around. It always seems like a good idea to have more digital storage, but then I have no clue what to do with it."

Dean chuckled. "That's how it goes. We appreciate that, Tommy. Now, we've just got some questions about your trip to Lake Henrietta. Was there anyone else around? Anyone you might've crossed paths with, even if it seemed benign?"

Tommy's focused expression returned. "I saw those two kids, the ones who were...killed."

Amelia leaned forward, elbows propped on her knees.

"What was their demeanor like? Did they seem nervous or scared to you at all?"

"No. They were just...normal, I guess. I've got a son and daughter who're in college, and to me, they were just a couple of normal college kids on a weekend outing. I passed them on one of the hiking trails, and we all just waved and said hi. I didn't think anything of it until I saw their pictures on the news."

As Tommy Mercer walked Amelia and Dean through his day of hiking and photography, Amelia's rush of anticipation at discovering a new lead began to wane. Aside from the first greeting, he hadn't come across Leslie or Jeremy again. He'd only run into a couple of locals who were out for a hike with their young children. While he provided their contact information, Amelia doubted they'd yield any useful information.

Using her work tablet, Amelia had Tommy show them on a map where he'd spent the night at Lake Henrietta. To her chagrin, he'd camped on the opposite side of the lake from Leslie and Jeremy.

Still, he could've witnessed something. Could Tommy have spotted them hauling the bodies to Lake Henrietta or one of its tributaries without even realizing it?

Amelia mentally crossed her fingers. "How about that night? Do you remember seeing or hearing anything once it got dark?"

"I'm not much of a night owl. It was probably around ten when I turned in for the night. All the fresh air really tuckers me out. I slept in the RV. Left the doors unlocked like I always do." Tommy scratched his bearded cheek. "Now, I do remember waking up in the middle of the night. That by itself isn't all that unusual since my wife passed, but I was sleeping with the windows open, and," he clasped his hands together and glanced from Amelia to Dean, "I swear I heard something out there, but I thought it was either an animal or something from my dream."

Dean scrawled out a few notes. "What did it sound like?"

"I don't know. A coyote. Or at least, that's what I thought it was. Coyotes make some pretty eerie sounds, you know? They don't sound like wolves like some folks think. They sound like women crying and screaming." His shoulders slumped as he let out a sigh. "That's probably not very helpful, is it? I just know I woke up and heard what I thought was a coyote. There was nothing after that, so I went back to sleep. I'm sorry."

Amelia held up her hand. Though she was disappointed they hadn't managed to chase down a viable lead, none of the situation was Tommy Mercer's fault. "There's no need to apologize. Do you know what time it was when you woke up?"

He brightened, apparently happy he had a concrete answer to one of Amelia's questions. "It was after one, one fifteen, I believe. I remember because I usually wake up around three, the witching hour, and I was surprised it was earlier than that."

"Thank you. We appreciate you coming forward and sparing some of your vacation time to talk to us."

With a wistful smile, Tommy clapped both hands on his knees and pushed to his feet. "Let me get that memory card for you before I forget. Hopefully, there'll be something helpful in one of those pictures I took."

As Mercer disappeared down a short hall, Dean straightened and pulled out his buzzing cell phone. He glanced at Amelia and flashed her the screen. "Sheriff's department."

A ray of hope pierced through Amelia's fog of disappointment, but she reminded herself not to get excited. Calls didn't always come with good news.

Dean tapped the screen and raised the phone to his ear. "Agent Steelman speaking."

Amelia couldn't make out the words of the tinny voice that responded, but Dean's expression grew stony.

"All right. Yeah, we're about done here. We'll be back at the department soon. Thanks. Bye." Pocketing the device, Dean turned back to Amelia. "Divers found two more bodies. They've also got brands on their skulls."

With the missing persons reports they'd uncovered, Amelia wasn't surprised to learn of the two new corpses, but she was still struck by a sense of unease. A resigned sigh escaped her. "For once, I wish we'd been wrong."

In the blink of an eye, thirty-six bodies had become thirty-eight.

17

Nearly a week had passed since my brother and I killed those sniveling brats, Jeremy Fitzgerald and Leslie Armstrong. I should've still been riding high on the exuberance of such a recent hunt, and maybe I was, but I was losing patience. Patience with my dying mother, my needy, weakling daughter, and my infuriating loser of a husband.

Grating my teeth, I set down my crossbow and pressed a button on the wall to reel in my most recent target. It was the second to last photo I had of my mother, and truth be told, I wished she looked more like this in the real world.

"You'd look so much better with a hole through your eye, Mother. I just wish I could put it there myself. These photographs only get me so close to the real thing, if you know what I mean."

Annoyance flared in my chest.

"Of course you don't know what I mean. You've lived your entire life worried about your appearance. That's the only reason you had kids. For appearances. As long as we looked like a wholesome little family, then politicians wouldn't be afraid to associate with you. They'd court you for donations, and you could throw your weight behind them so they'd pass legislation to give your business a fat tax cut. That's all your children ever were to you."

I couldn't lie to myself, though. I'd had my daughter for precisely the same reason. My parents hounded my brother and me to give them grandchildren, and for years, I had no idea why.

So they could treat them like second-class citizens too? Or did they want another shot at raising us?

As it turned out, they actually liked their grandchildren. They'd paid attention to them. Maybe old age got to them sooner than I'd expected.

I'd never understood why they doted on my pathetic daughter. If the girl had lived under my mother's care like I had, she'd have thrown herself into traffic before her thirteenth birthday.

I stabbed my index finger through the hole in my mother's eye, imagining it was the inside of her skull on the other side.

The *click* of the door unlocking ripped my focus away from the old bat's picture.

Garrett.

Not expecting him and not particularly happy to see him.

For the past two days, my dear twin brother had gone MIA. It wasn't the first time he'd dropped off the face of the planet after one of our hunts, but that didn't make me any less uneasy about his absence.

I'd always been the levelheaded twin, whereas this guy... well, he never really knew when to stop pushing his luck.

Tossing aside the photo, I jabbed a finger at him as the door closed. "Where the fuck have you been? For all I knew, you'd taken off to Uruguay in your fancy little Cessna."

A shit-eating grin spread over his face. "I could've, huh? But that fancy little Cessna is how we've gotten all around the country over the years to satisfy your itch, so don't hate. Can you imagine if we'd dropped all those bodies in Chicago or anywhere in the state? I wouldn't take off with the plane. Duh." He made a show of fanning himself. "Even the dumbass bumpkin cops would've caught on."

I waved away his remark like an annoying bug. "Fine, but that's not my point. Where in the hell have you been? Don't tell me..."

By the mischievous look on his face, I already knew what was coming next.

"You've got to be kidding me." Irritation sawed at the last thread of my patience. "I've been here in Chicago dealing with our half-dead bitch of a mother, and you've been..." I paused to feign contemplation. "Oh, right. You've been out dicking around by Lake Henrietta, admiring your handiwork, haven't you?"

"Hold on. You're going to be happy I went back there. Trust me." He pulled out his cell, tapping it a few times before he held it out for me.

On the screen, a man stood beside a tall maple. His worn jeans, work boots, and plaid button-down were consistent with the fashion sense of ninety percent of the state of Illinois.

But when I zoomed in on the image, his vivid-blue eyes showed a sharp intelligence. With brown hair brushed straight back from his face, designer sunglasses on his head, and a state-of-the-art camera in his grasp, it didn't take much to discern a difference in him from the typical sheriff's deputies I'd grown accustomed to over the years.

Once I'd had a chance to study the man, my brother swiped over to a second picture, this one of a woman. Like the man, she stood in the middle of the woods. Her plain gray t-shirt, skinny jeans, and boots were unremarkable, but the way the blond at the tips of her hair melded into the dark brown was flawless. I'd been to my share of hair stylists over the years, and I knew how easy it was to screw up a balayage. Her eyes were just as astute as the man's in the previous photo, and the camera around her neck was high-end like his.

I turned my attention back to my brother. "These people are investigating those two kids?"

My brother's suave smile returned as he pocketed his cell. "They sure are. They were out there working with the deputies, but I think they're gone now."

"They're Feds." My remark wasn't a question. We'd dealt with federal agents on a couple separate occasions, most recently in Minnesota.

Well, *I* hadn't dealt with any Feds. My daredevil brother, on the other hand, had skulked around in the shadows to observe them.

Garrett crossed his arms. "They are. From the Chicago field office. Basically our own backyard. It's probably where they are right now."

I hated feeding into my brother's risky behavior, but he was right—I did want to know more about these agents. The idea of watching them as they tried and failed to figure out who killed those people at Lake Henrietta sent a delightful shiver down my spine.

They weren't our usual targets, but there was a first time for everything.

I sighed. "Do you know their names?"

"I overheard their last names, but not their first. The woman is Storm, and the man is Steelman." His eyes glittered in the same malevolent way they did when we were about to close in on our prey. "Wouldn't that be the thrill of a lifetime? Hunting two people from the FBI. That'd be the ultimate test."

He made an excellent point. We'd stuck to civilians so far, but there had to be some way we could raise the stakes...

No, not right now. Not until after I was finished dealing with our insufferable mother. And, of course, our older brother. He'd arrive in Chicago any day now, and odds were, he'd be pissed with the agreement my mother had made with me.

As Garrett opened his mouth to speak, I cut him off with an upraised hand. "You obviously don't know this yet, but Eddie'll be here today or tomorrow."

"What?" His face screwed up in a combination of rage and unease. "Why? Because Mom's dying? I thought you said she agreed to give you most of Eddie's inheritance if you took care of her while she was sick?"

"She did, but Eddie's still coming. You know how he is. When he finds out that old bat is giving me half of his share, only God knows what he'll try to pull. We're talking about more than fifty million. He won't take that well."

With a scoff, Garrett shook his head. "So what do we do?"

I flashed him a sarcastic smile. "That's what I've been trying to figure out while you were screwing around with the Feds. Remember how we used to torture him when we were kids? Hell, we fucked him up so bad, he ended up addicted to painkillers. Too bad he didn't overdose." The thought of my older brother lying blue on the floor of his bathroom next to an empty pill bottle warmed my heart. "I think we need to get rid of him. Make it look like an accident."

"An accident. I like the simplicity of it. People have accidents all the time when they're traveling. Or maybe he wound up in the wrong part of the city and got carjacked or mugged. We can just blame it on the city's crime rate. Something like that. Heck, we could even have him relapse into the clutches of his addiction. Make it look like Mom's death was too much to handle. We've just got to get him alone."

Daredevil or not, my twin had the same knack for problem-solving I did.

We'd kept Eddie under control for most our lives, and we'd figure out how to rein him in now.

Once he was dealt with, we'd revisit hunting those two Feds.

18

Tapping a ballpoint pen against the heel of her hand, Amelia leaned back in her chair with a *creak*. She and Dean had arrived back in Chicago late last night after spending more than two days in Henrietta City. Then, a bit early in the morning for Amelia's taste, Sheriff Bradley had called to say they'd finally located Leslie's Hampton's car parked over two miles away from where the couple set up their campsite. Before Amelia or Dean could get excited about the find, Bradley said the car revealed nothing new beyond Leslie's excellent selection of metal music.

Since that call, Amelia and Dean had scrawled dates, locations, and names across their enormous whiteboard until their hands started to cramp. They just lacked anything else to go on yet.

TGIF?

Not for them. They'd be working the weekend for sure.

Dean paused where he'd been pacing back and forth in front of the window. "Well, other than confirming the identities of Kayla and Otto Hampton, the interview with their family members didn't give us much. Both of them were average folks who liked to spend time in the outdoors."

In addition to the Hamptons, the lab also identified one set of skeletal remains via dental records. Angie Marsh's parents had reported her missing nearly three years ago after she and her good friend, Ron Dawson, had gone on a camping trip together. Ron's dental records weren't on file, but a wedding ring—complete with an engraved message from his husband—had been found on his body.

Despite the decomposition of Kayla and Otto Hampton, their families had still managed to identify them.

Though Amelia and Dean had gone through the painstaking process of reaching out to the rest of the victims' family members, they'd gleaned zero useful information.

When the Duluth field office handed over their case files, which dated back nearly a decade, Amelia and Dean used most of the whiteboard to list all the victims. Fortunately, all of them had been identified so far.

They still needed to meet with Layton Redker from the Behavioral Analysis Unit. In the meantime, they scanned through the crimes again in hopes they'd pick out a pattern they'd missed the first hundred times.

Amelia turned her focus back to the board. Leaning forward, she propped her elbows atop the table. "The victims are from all over the country, so it's unlikely they'll be connected to one another. If they were, I think we'd have already picked up on the pattern."

"Or someone else would have."

"Right."

Dean resumed his pacing. "Raphael and Caroline Warren were the first victims, both from Saint Louis, Missouri. They were killed nine years and eleven months ago, clear down by Chillicothe National Forest. The coroner estimated they'd been submerged for six days before they were found. The Wilhelmina County Sheriff's Department worked the case, but it went cold within a month."

"And then the next victims, Tracy McCall and Brad Petty, were killed the following summer in Lower Michigan, in Ludington, along the coast of Lake Michigan. The gap between the Warrens and the Ludington case is fourteen months, but then the next victims were killed nine months later. And ever since then, the gap has gotten smaller. Especially now, with only a couple weeks between the Hamptons and Leslie Armstrong and Jeremy Fitzgerald."

"Not to mention, the last two sets of victims are," he held up a finger, "A, in the exact same location, and B, both in the same location as a murder from three years ago. Which is where Agent Redker and the BAU come into play. Something significant is happening to these killers right now, but we don't know for sure what it is."

"Okay. And in the case notes for each of these older double homicides, there's some indication that two killers were present too." Amelia didn't care what the killers' external stressor was. All she cared about was stopping them before more people died. "There are also notes from interviews with potential witnesses in several of the cases who claim they may or may not have heard a sound that may or may not have resembled a scream."

Despite Amelia's flat tone, or perhaps because of it, Dean grinned. "I know that feeling. Everything's clear as mud, isn't it? It sure makes me wish I could go back in time and sit in on the investigations myself. Not that I think any of those folks were doing a bad job. I'm sure they did their best, but you know what they say about two heads being better than one. Plus, a double homicide isn't exactly something the sheriff's deputies expect out in the middle of nowhere."

His assessment of Amelia's frustration was spot-on. She didn't doubt the competency of her fellow investigators, but two heads were indeed much better than one, especially when one of the heads was trained and experienced in homicide investigations.

"True. People can fall off cliffs, drown, and who knows what else while out in the woods. You wouldn't just assume a serial killer was on the loose."

Along with witnesses at several of the sites stating they'd potentially heard a scream in the middle of the night, every other piece of information was so damn close to being useful but still led them nowhere.

Holding in a sigh, Amelia propped her chin on one hand. "If you were camping and woke up to someone screaming in the wilderness at night, what would you do?"

"I'm not the best person to ask about it since I'm a trained FBI agent, just like you. I know we'd do something, but you can't look at it from our perspective. What would Joe Schmo do? Would he even recognize it as a human's scream, or would he think it was an animal, like Tommy Mercer did?"

"Good point. Folks out camping are way more worried about wild animals than they are about being a potential witness to, or victim of, a serial killer. Well, normal folks anyway. Like Tommy said, some animals sound an awful lot like people." A pang of sympathy jabbed at Amelia. She could only imagine how guilty some of the witnesses must've felt when they learned they might've overheard a person screaming for help. "It's not their fault. These sick bastards have been doing this for almost a decade. They probably know most people will either dismiss the screams as animal noises or choose not to get involved."

Dean paused again, his gaze drifting to the whiteboard. "Yeah, more than likely. I think it's a natural reaction for people to not rush toward potential danger. You and I have had the training, both by the military and the Bureau, so we run toward the threat while everyone else runs in the other direction. I can't really blame them."

Maybe the killers count on that reaction. Prey on people's fears and the notion that, when in doubt, no one does anything.

Odds were, if this pair of killers had been operating for nearly a decade under the radar, they were intelligent. Amelia straightened in her chair and drummed her fingers along the armrest. "What do you want to bet they've been picking these isolated locations for more than one reason?"

Dean cocked his head to one side. "What're you thinking?"

"Aside from the obvious isolation, I think it's highly likely they're counting on people being too afraid to intervene. If that's the case, then it stands to reason they're probably aware of some basic facts about law enforcement."

"Right."

"So their decision to target people in isolated, underpopulated areas is calculated for more than one reason. They know the jurisdiction will most likely fall on the county. Take Jordan County, for example. Their population is around twenty thousand. Obviously, like we saw, the department puts their very best into what they do, but they won't have staff with the same level of expertise as the FBI."

Dean nodded. "I see what you're saying. It's why they dump the bodies in lakes too. They probably know the corpses will be found eventually, just like they know the sheriff's department will investigate the murders to the best of their ability."

"But," Amelia held out her hands, "they also know everything they're doing will slow down the investigation. We've got nineteen pairs of victims that've been found so far, for thirty-eight total murders. Of those nineteen pairs, only seven were found within a week of their deaths. Another seven were found within a month, and the remaining five weren't found for more than six months after they were killed."

"Plus, in all that time underwater, most, if not all, trace evidence was washed away." Dean crossed his arms and looked at the whiteboard like it owed him money. "And then they know the sheriff's departments will be stretched thin trying to dredge up the bodies from the bottom of the lake. Hell, it took years for the Bureau to get involved. How many times has this case changed hands now? It's like a morbid version of *The Sisterhood of the Traveling Pants*."

Amelia's nose twitched in confusion. "What?"

"You know. The case file is the pants."

"It's...something like that, yeah." Amelia tried not to dwell on her partner's bizarre film reference. He did not strike her as a chick flick kind of guy. "There's also one thing I noticed about all the victims, something that might be a common thread. It could be why the killers are targeting them. From what we can tell, most of them are keen on the outdoors, but none of them are locals. The killers seem to be picking people who're from out of the county or even the state."

"That's true." Rubbing his chin, Dean rocked back and forth from the balls of his feet to his heels. "It makes sense if you think about it like a serial killer would. The murder of a person from out of town doesn't make nearly as much of a splash as the murder of a member of the community. Leslie and Jeremy lived in Waterloo, which wasn't too far away, but still. No one knew who they were. I think the department would've acted differently if they were dealing with the murders of their neighbors."

"How, though?" Amelia rolled a pen back and forth across the tabletop but stopped when she realized her rhythm matched Dean's rocking. "How do they know their victims are from out of town?"

His expression tightened. "They've got to be stalking them. Either that, or they interact with the vics somewhere along the way. How many times have you been on vacation and had someone in a gas station or a restaurant ask where you're from? It's pretty common small talk."

Another reason I hate small talk.

"Is there any way we can use this?" Amelia suspected she already knew the answer to her question, but at this point, she and Dean were spitballing. "Like, could we pull security camera footage from gas stations nearby, or..." She trailed off, heaving a sigh as she slumped down in her chair. "No, that wouldn't work. We'd need to have some idea of what we were looking for, otherwise it'd be useless. We'd be searching for a needle in the bottom of the Mariana Trench."

"Plus, we already checked Jeremy's and Leslie's financial records. There were no purchases from anywhere in Henrietta City. They probably fueled up before they left home, then planned to stop at a gas station on their way back to Waterloo."

"So we're back to the stalking, then." Amelia couldn't decide if the killers stalking their victims to glean information was more or less unsettling than acquiring it in a casual conversation.

Sure, plenty of serial killers followed their victims to learn their routines and find an opening to attack, but there was something especially unnerving about picturing two psychopaths skulking around in the woods, circling Jeremy and Leslie like a couple of predatory big cats.

Only these weren't jaguars or leopards, animals that hunted to survive. They weren't even coyotes.

No, these were two cold-blooded murderers who'd racked up a body count nearing forty, and who'd add to that number if they weren't stopped.

19

While they waited for their meeting with Agent Redker, Amelia got a call from Dr. Adam Francis, the forensic pathologist, to let her know that he and Dr. Sabrina Ackerly, the medical examiner, had completed their postmortem exams of the six victims from Lake Henrietta. Amelia and Dean took off to meet with the pathologist. Fortunately, the M.E.'s office wasn't far from the FBI building, so trips back and forth were no issue.

With the sun high in the sky, Amelia stepped out of the black SUV and stretched her arms as she waited for Dean. She wondered if her muscles would ever stop feeling sore again. It'd been a long time since boot camp.

No matter how often she visited the Cook County Medical Examiner's Office, she never got over its fortress-like appearance. The building's concrete walls were interspersed with long, narrow windows tinted the eerie shade of nighttime. In Amelia's opinion, it looked more like a prison than a medical office.

After she and Dean signed in at the front desk, they headed downstairs to the exam rooms. All six victims had been positively identified either via family members, dental records, personal effects, or a combination of the three. Though having the victims' identities was a huge step in the right direction, there was still a litany of puzzle pieces left to put in place.

At least all the notifications had been made and families could begin traveling the long road of grief and healing. Not for the first time for many of them.

As Amelia followed Dean to a door at the end of a brightly lit hall, she mentally crossed her fingers for a new piece of information.

They shoved their way through the swinging double doors, revealing a spacious room with square metal drawers decorating three walls. Dr. Francis's brown eyes flicked up from his clipboard, a smile brightening his face. Despite his bald head and the flecks of white in his goatee, the lines on his dark skin were minimal. "Hello, Agents. Nice to see you again. I'm glad you could make it here so quickly."

Despite the bleak subject matter, Amelia couldn't help but return Dr. Francis's smile. The forensic pathologist gave off a fatherly vibe that set those around him at ease. As far as Amelia was concerned, it was an underrated quality in such a grim field. "No problem. We appreciate you and Dr. Ackerly getting through all these exams in such a timely manner."

"We do our best. I realize this is quite a large case, so we wanted to ensure you had as much information as possible as quickly as we could get it to you." His expression sobered as he glanced down at the clipboard. "I've sent you digital copies of our reports, so you can review everything when you're back at the field office."

"Thank you." Dean's stony focus matched Dr. Francis's. "What did you learn from the autopsies?"

The forensic pathologist flipped through a couple pages. "I'm afraid all the trace evidence was washed away by the lake, even from the two most recent vics."

Though the news was disappointing, Amelia wasn't surprised. "We figured that was the case. What can you tell us about the causes of death?"

"I'll start with Angie Marsh and Ron Dawson, since they were the first two killed. Both bodies were skeletal remains, but the divers were quite thorough and managed to retrieve many of their bones. As our preliminary report already stated, Angie Marsh was identified via dental records provided by her family, and Ron Dawson's engraved wedding ring was found on his body. Both skulls had marks along the frontal and parietal bones that were consistent with the removal of the scalp."

Amelia recalled similar notes from the postmortems of the victims from nearly ten years ago. "That's the same as the previous case notes. That would mean the pattern of injuries has been consistent for almost a decade."

"It would seem so. I compared my notes with some of the older cases, and, well..." Glancing from Amelia to Dean, Dr. Francis lifted a shoulder. "These six are incredibly similar to the victims from the other scenes. However, we have some context that many of the others were missing. The crossbow bolt."

Dean lifted an eyebrow. "There was a broken crossbow bolt found about five years ago in southern Wisconsin. Only a piece of the bolt was stuck in the lung of one of the victims, and the investigators speculated it might've broken off *before* the victim died. Otherwise, aside from the one we found, there haven't been any others."

"That's accurate." Dr. Francis tapped his clipboard. "But when I looked closer at these injuries, such as the one at the base of Angie Marsh's skull, all the puncture wounds are consistent with a powerful crossbow. It seems the weapon was a mystery for quite a while, until the crossbow bolt was found in Wisconsin. Plenty of the postmortem exams *speculated* that the injuries were sustained from an bolt of some sort, but the case in Wisconsin was proof."

"And the bolt the techs found at Lake Henrietta proves for sure the murder weapon was a crossbow."

Dr. Francis pointed at Amelia. "Right you are. It appears, much like those who pick up their shell casings, or 'police their brass,' the killers in these cases removed the crossbow bolts before dumping the bodies."

"Yet this time they didn't." Dean didn't direct his comment at anyone so much as he muttered to himself while checking his notebook. "Everything you said aligns with what Dr. Islas speculated out at Lake Henrietta."

Maybe this meant the shooter was getting sloppy. Though Amelia wanted to allow herself a moment of hope, she'd experienced enough disappointment in past cases to know she should temper her reaction to this news.

Different was good, and the crossbow bolt being found was good, but crossbows weren't the same as firearms. Where a bullet could be linked to a particular gun via a ballistics exam—each gun barrel left unique markings on bullets and, in some cases, even on shell casings—a crossbow bolt had no such unique identifier. They might find DNA that could prove useful, of course, but not as immediately so as a bullet.

These killers were, indeed, smart to avoid weapons with such common pitfalls for killers.

Amelia and Dean and all the investigators helping with this case would just have to be smarter.

"Anyway," Dr. Francis waved a hand, "that's all more in

your area of expertise than mine. Now, Angie Marsh and Ron Dawson's causes of death are difficult to say for certain. Ms. Marsh was likely killed by the crossbow bolt that punctured the bottom of her occipital bone, but there was another wound on one of her ribs to indicate a bolt hit her in the lung as well. Chances are, when she sustained the fatal injury to her head, she was already in bad shape."

Dean frowned, leaning forward a little, as if eager to latch onto this new pattern. "Another lung shot. It's almost like the perp aims for the chest to slow the victim down, then fires the fatal shot to the head."

Though Amelia was no hunter herself, she'd heard stories from others about techniques for hunting deer, including hitting the body behind the foreleg—the location of the heart and lungs—before finishing it off. The crossbow killer's method sounded similar.

Dr. Francis offered Dean a nod. "I was under the same impression. Ron Dawson, on the other hand, doesn't appear to have been shot with the crossbow. However, there was a deep mark along his C-four vertebra." He turned his head to the side and pointed to his neck just beneath the chin. "That's the bone in your spine that lines up with this part of your throat."

In a flash, the image of the gaping wound beneath Leslie Armstrong's chin appeared in Amelia's mind. Whoever slit her throat had cut so deeply, they'd damn near decapitated her. "His throat was slit?"

"Correct. That injury is consistent across all nineteen cases, isn't it?"

"Yeah. There's always one victim whose throat was slit, and then, apparently, the other one is killed with a crossbow." Amelia's stomach sank a little more as she recounted the pattern she and Dean had stared at for multiple days straight now. Smart, but also ruthless. She couldn't think about how if they didn't succeed where many other law enforcement departments hadn't, more pairs of victims would die these gruesome deaths.

Dr. Francis tapped his clipboard. "Kayla and Otto Hampton sustained the same injuries, though theirs were more obvious due to the lessened state of decomposition. We estimate their bodies were in the water for at least a few weeks. Otto Hampton was shot twice in the chest with what we believe was a crossbow, and then once at the base of the skull. Kayla Hampton's throat was slit much like Leslie Armstrong's, and she also sustained a laceration to the side, right below her ribs, and another on the side of her knee, right above the fibula."

There weren't many fates more terrifying than being ambushed in the middle of the night by a killer with a massive knife. In fact, the situation was so frightening, there were a multitude of horror films based on that very scenario.

Kayla and Otto Hampton, along with Leslie Armstrong, Jeremy Fitzgerald, Angie Marsh, and Ron Dawson, had been subjected to a real-life horror movie.

Before she could let herself imagine the terror the victims must have felt in their final moments, Amelia cleared her throat to bring herself back to reality, refusing to let her mind wander down that path with so much work yet to be done. "That brings us to Leslie and Jeremy."

"They were in far better shape than the other victims found at Lake Henrietta." Though Dr. Francis's expression had remained neutral throughout his summary, a shadow passed behind his eyes. Maybe seeing the results of humans hunted just for sport on recent victims took its toll, even on forensic pathologists who witnessed a parade of mutilated bodies every day.

Somehow, that halted Amelia's sinking into despair. So long as at least one person empathized with murder victims, humanity still stood a chance. She straightened her shoulders as he continued.

"Jeremy Fitzgerald sustained two crossbow shots, and Leslie Armstrong was killed when her carotid artery was severed. I also found contusions around the sphenoid and temporal bones. The blows were forceful enough to damage the bones and cause swelling in the brain. It's likely she was unconscious when she was killed, and even if her throat hadn't been slit, she'd have died without emergency medical intervention to relieve the swelling in her brain."

A crease formed between Dean's eyebrows. "With that kind of damage, the perp would've had to use a blunt weapon, right? A rock or something?"

Dr. Francis peered down at his notes and pursed his lips. "Based on the size of the contusion, namely the fact that it was smaller than a human fist, I'm leaning toward the use of a weapon. Though it could've been a rock, I think if we take everything in context, it's more likely the perp used the hilt of their blade."

So it wasn't enough for them to beat Leslie into a coma. The sick bastard slit her throat and then scalped her.

Before Amelia could respond, her cell buzzed in the pocket of her jacket. Holding up a hand to Dean and Dr. Francis, she pulled it out. A jolt of anticipation rushed through her as she glanced at the screen. "Hold on. I'd better take this. It's forensics."

Dean's back straightened at the announcement, even though Dr. Francis seemed unfazed.

Swiping the screen, Amelia raised the device to her ear. "This is Agent Storm."

"Agent Storm, hello. This is Caroline Haldin with the forensic lab. I thought you'd want to hear this information right away. We've finished processing the crossbow bolt found at the Lake Henrietta crime scene."

Amelia's skin tingled like she was in the midst of an electrical storm. "Did you find anything?"

"We did." Caroline chuckled lightly. "You're not going to believe this, but we found a usable fingerprint."

Amelia crossed her fingers, unable to squelch a tiny flare of hope, even though she knew she should. "Were there any matches in the database?"

"None, unfortunately."

Even still, Amelia wasn't disappointed—learning the perpetrator didn't have a record registered in the national database wasn't a huge surprise. With the care the two killers had put into orchestrating their crimes over the last decade, she'd have been amazed if their vicious crime spree was coming to an end thanks to a single errant fingerprint.

Regardless of whether they could put a name to the print, this was still a tremendous piece of evidence—more than enough to refill any of the determination Amelia had lost with their dead ends.

With their case taking shape at last, she'd keep hunting these hunters until they tracked down a suspect who matched that fingerprint.

20

With two fresh iced lattes in hand, Amelia elbowed the lever handle to her and Dean's incident room and stepped inside. Fresh from their trip to the morgue, she blinked to adjust her vision to the brightness of the sunny space.

"Afternoon, Agent Storm." At his seat at the table inside, Layton Redker lifted a hand to greet her, the corners of his eyes creasing with his smile. Despite the first hints of silver in his dark hair, Layton's modest faux hawk, along with the lack of lines on his clean-shaven face, lent him a youthful aesthetic. "Nice to see you again."

Amelia passed one of the lattes to Dean and shrugged her handbag off her shoulder. Though she'd worked with Layton on several cases in the past, she didn't know much about him outside of his professional credentials. Not that he had any shortage of those. Approximately six months ago, Layton had transitioned from his role in Cyber Crimes to the BAU.

It seemed like a strange transfer at first, but apparently, Layton had spent the last several years acquiring his doctorate in psychology. Not many of the agents in the BAU went as far as obtaining a PhD, so his level of education alone made him stand out.

Pulling out a chair, Amelia set down her latte. "It's nice to see you too. Please, call me Amelia. I feel like your little sister, I see you so often. How have you been?"

"Can't complain." Layton lifted a shoulder. "I, uh...just got back from a camping trip with my daughter, actually."

Dean halted midway through unwrapping his straw. "You did *what* now?"

Amelia wasn't sure if she should laugh or relay her relief that Layton and his kid were still alive.

"I'm fine, don't worry. Ironic, though." Redker pulled a rueful face as he set a water bottle next to his laptop. "I've got a pretty nice RV my uncle left me when he passed a few years ago, so I try to make use of it, even though I'm not much of an outdoorsman. Honestly, that might be why he left it to me. As some kind of posthumous joke. Which, if you knew him, you'd probably think was funny."

In that single statement, Amelia was confident she'd just learned more about Layton Redker, the man, than she'd uncovered thus far in all their interactions.

"Anyway, enough about that." Layton opened his laptop. "I'm sure you can imagine my surprise when I read through this case file. I wasn't anywhere near Lake Henrietta, but it was still...disconcerting. Especially considering these perps are targeting pairs of people."

Probably feels like you dodged a bullet.

Then again, Amelia wasn't sure how well the killers would have fared if they'd made the mistake of trying to ambush a seasoned FBI agent. As she and Dean had surmised earlier, the perps were likely too smart to go after a federal agent and his kid. They'd draw unwanted attention to their actions too.

"I guess we can start there." Dean cleared his throat. "We've got a pair of serials, active for almost ten years. There've been serial killer duos in the past, but they aren't all that common. What'd you make of that?"

"Well, I've got a couple takeaways. First, there were no signs of sexual assault on any of the thirty-eight victims." Layton tapped some keys on his laptop and glanced at Amelia and Dean. "Although, we can't be one hundred percent sure when it comes to the bodies that are badly decomposed."

Amelia followed his line of thinking. "But with no evidence of sexual assault on any of the other vics, it's likely the killers adhered to the same pattern."

"Exactly."

"So they're not killing for sexual gratification?"

"I don't think so, no." Layton readjusted his black-rimmed glasses. "The pursuit of sexual gratification and control is one of the most common motives for serial killers, and that's also true when you look at romantic couples who kill together, though there are other factors we'll need to examine."

Amelia leaned forward, nodding. "Oh, like the Moorhouse Murders in Australia. Catherine Birnie left her husband and six kids to be with her old flame. She and David Birnie abducted five girls, and they raped and killed four of them. The fifth managed to get away and ultimately led the police back to the Birnies' house."

She would never understand how a woman, much less a mother, could aid in such monstrous acts.

Layton bobbed his head in agreement. "Then there are couples like lonely hearts killers, who commit murders for financial gain. Those are less common but still a popular motive for serial killer couples. On the other hand, there are serial killer pairs who aren't romantically involved. In many cases, these killers are related, usually siblings."

A scent of vanilla floated on the air as Dean pulled the lid off his latte. "Makes sense, I guess. You'd have to have a lot of rapport with someone if you trusted them to have your back in a murdering spree."

"That's the reason for it, more or less." Layton reached for his bottle of water, crinkling the plastic beneath his grip.

"Then for this case, we can safely rule out a financial or sexual motive." Amelia scratched lines through some of her initial hypotheses written in her notebook. "Jeremy Fitzgerald and Leslie Armstrong were a couple of broke college kids, and none of their credit cards were missing."

Dean pointed at Amelia in agreement as he swirled his latte with his straw. "Kayla and Otto Hampton were both buried in student loan debt. Their friends and family said they went camping because it was the only type of vacation they could afford. And in one of the older cases, Kasey and Will Minnick down in Louisiana, the local cops found several hundred dollars in Kasey's purse at their campsite."

"Okay." Layton leaned back in his chair and twisted off the cap of his water bottle. "Motive isn't financial, and it isn't sexual. That leaves us with thrill-seeking as the most likely candidate. Which, when you take it in context with every other aspect of these murders, seems to fit. Stalking the victims, scaring the hell out of them in the middle of the night, hunting them through the woods...these are all consistent with perps chasing a dopamine rush or living out some twisted fantasy."

Fantasizing about murdering innocent people in the woods at night struck Amelia's Organized Crime-centered brain as foreign. No profit or clout came from killing college students in the sticks of Illinois. No one had ordered a hit on Jeremy Fitzpatrick or the others. In a twisted way, mafiosos didn't seem so terrible compared to the David and Catherine Birnies of the world. At least their motives made sense.

Surprised at that conclusion, Amelia pursed her lips, focusing on Layton before she started favoring the kinds of people she'd seen ruin many lives for money and power. "What do you make of the locations? Serial killers typically have a hunting ground, correct?"

"Typically, yes." After a quick pull at his water, Layton returned the bottle to the table and turned his laptop around. "Here's a quick map I put together of all the sites. The outliers are pretty clear, with California being the farthest, followed by Louisiana and Colorado. Otherwise, they're all in the Midwest and nearby. Michigan, Minnesota, Wisconsin, Ohio, Indiana, Missouri, northern Arkansas, northwestern Tennessee. You get the picture."

Dean squinted at the tiny laptop screen, making Amelia wonder if that was why Layton needed glasses. "Even if they're nomadic, they might be from somewhere in the Midwest, which is why so many of the victims were found around here."

"That's what I was thinking." Layton spun his laptop to face him again. "But serial killer or not, people still have to make money to survive. In this context, that can mean one of two things. Either the perps work a job that involves frequent travel or relocation, such as long-haul trucking or even working as a pilot or flight attendant. Or they come from money, and they don't have to work. Based on how they select their targets, these are definitely organized killers."

Amelia recalled one of her first lessons in serial killers—organized versus disorganized. Where disorganized killers were often driven by urges they couldn't control, organized killers meticulously planned and orchestrated the murders of their victims.

Despite the popular myth, serial killers, on average, weren't any more or less intelligent than the general population. However, there was a slight deficit in intelligence when comparing disorganized serial killers to their organized counterparts.

Layton set aside his laptop. "That brings me to the next point. It's clear they're making an effort to conceal or destroy evidence as they go, hence their dumping the victims into a nearby body of water. I do wonder if it has any real significance beyond a forensic countermeasure, and I think it might."

"You have a theory?" Dean took a long drink of his latte.

"Possibly. There could be an emotional connection, maybe something that happened when they were younger that they're seeking to replicate. Or it might be some form of baptism for their victims. It could even be simpler. They could be disposing of the bodies in rivers and lakes because they want the water to wash away evidence without washing away the body."

A chill crept down Amelia's spine. "They want the bodies to be found."

"Yes. If you ask me, there's no question about it. Why go through the trouble of carving the same symbol onto all the victims' skulls? They know the carving will be preserved even if the bodies are underwater for years. They're making sure we know they did all this."

"Maybe that's the wealth aspect of the Fehu symbol." Dean ran a thoughtful finger through the condensation ring his plastic cup left behind on the wood veneer. "They see these kills as their property. It's like they're signing a check."

"And waving the check around for everyone to see, only with people's lives." The more Layton divulged of his report, the more Amelia got the sense of these killers as rich, uncaring assholes.

Layton briefly dislodged his glasses as he scratched his nose. "Since it's their signature, one they're psychologically compelled to complete, if a kill were interrupted and they didn't get to mark their victims, that could generate a stressor that drives them to kill again almost immediately."

"That means the marking is just as important to them as the act of killing."

"I think so, yeah."

Whether she worked in Violent Crime or Organized Crime, Amelia realized, killers shared some striking similarities. Mafiosos who gunned down others over territorial disputes or other perceived slights left behind their handiwork to serve as proof that no one messed with them.

Serial killers like to do that too.

No matter the type of crime Amelia investigated, it all boiled down to one ridiculous dick-measuring contest.

She sighed. "What's your take on the scalping, then? Do you think they did it specifically so they could carve the rune onto the victims' skulls?"

"Maybe." Layton picked at the label of his water. "But scalping's been used throughout history for a variety of reasons. Here at home, some Native American tribes took scalps as trophies, often proving a warrior's accomplishments. There could be more significance to the perps choosing to scalp their victims, but it's difficult to pinpoint. Same goes for the rune, Fehu. The significance could be in the rune itself, or it could be in what the rune symbolizes."

"Wealth or property, like we talked about." Amelia stirred her drink with the straw, trying to remix the melting ice water with the coffee. "But also cattle or sheep. Which still goes back to the property thing."

"More than likely, the perps view their victims as less than, so to them, they're akin to livestock. So...right." Layton blinked up at the overhead lights, seeming to consider that a moment. "That leads me to believe they view themselves as a cut above the rest of humanity. Both of them likely display narcissistic tendencies coupled with a substantial lack of empathy. These traits don't spring up overnight, though, so chances are good these two have menaced society since they were young."

If anything, Dean's expression turned even stonier. "And based on the fact that they've been killing people for almost ten years, they've probably got an entire graveyard's worth of skeletons in their closets."

"There's no doubt about that." Layton gestured at the jam-packed whiteboard.

Could there be more victims without the Fehu rune? Would we even know? Amelia's stomach twisted at that idea, but she decided against voicing it. If evidence of more without this link surfaced, they'd really have their hands full. For now, they'd stick with the connections they'd already made.

"Considering these murders started so long ago, that should put both perps in their mid-thirties." Layton glanced at the laptop by his side, referring to a note. "They're probably not much older than forty, though, given the level of sociopathy and narcissism present. I think they started killing when they were fairly young. And based on the niche weapons they're using, as well as the quality of the intact crossbow bolt, I'm leaning more toward concluding they're people of means as opposed to nomads."

What could have possibly occurred in the lives of not one but *two* people to result in such an unsettling disregard for human life?

"Thinking of that..." Little puffs of air sounded as Amelia thumbed through her notebook to an earlier page. "The lab just informed us they got a usable fingerprint off the bolt found out at Lake Henrietta. We'll need to chase down whether there's anything unique about the bolt itself."

As if digging his way out of his own grim conclusions, Dean straightened his shoulders. "How about motive? Do you have any theories about what could be compelling these two to kill over and over?"

Layton glanced back and forth between Amelia and Dean. "Actually, I do have a theory. It's just an idea that came to me when I was reading over the forensic report about the murder weapons. A crossbow isn't a very common murder weapon, and the only time I really hear about one being used is for hunting. Taking the scalping and the Fehu rune into consideration...I think they're hunting their victims."

"I think you're right." Validation of her own theory brought a grim smile to Amelia's face. She knew the story of Robert Hansen and how he hunted his victims like animals. It was a twisted concept she'd hoped was relegated to the remote confines of Alaska, but that hope kept right on waning. "They're not the only hunters out here, though."

Across from her, a spark lit in Dean's eyes as they shared a look. Even if Amelia didn't have Zane at her side, she recognized at once that Dean would bring just as much drive to this case. They *would* catch these people.

However highly these so-called hunters thought of themselves, Amelia planned to lock them up like the animals they distained.

21

Though I'd intended to spend the day at home crafting a plan to deal with my older brother, my afternoon was interrupted by the call I'd been waiting to receive for weeks.

"I'm so sorry. Your mother suffered a series of strokes this morning and passed away."

Each time I repeated the nurse's solemn words in my head, I had to fight to keep a giddy smile off my face. Finally, that wretched woman was gone. No more of her nagging me to have some deep discussion about all the wrongs she'd done me.

How could she think a conversation now, more than twenty years after the fact, could help anything? It couldn't. The only reason she'd even tried to mend fences with me was to make herself seem like a better person.

My healing never factored into her equation.

I knew the truth. I knew what a witch she really was, even if she tried to coddle my daughter in some pitiful attempt to reconcile with me. She was finally, blissfully gone, and unless her ghost had the ability to alter legal documents, I was about to come into a large inheritance.

All that was left was to accompany my brothers to a meeting with the lawyer so my twin and I could finally collect what was rightfully ours. As long as Eddie didn't attempt some legal chicanery to pull the rug out from beneath us, life would be good.

Hopefully, he'd just take his reduced portion of our parents' fortune and slither back to Colorado.

No matter. I wouldn't let thoughts of my older brother derail my good spirits. With the warmth of the sun greeting me when I stepped out the front door, I left my worries on the porch as I advanced toward a sleek SUV at the curb. My driver was waiting.

The relief was palpable. My shoulders were lighter as I climbed into the back seat of the private car, and try as I might, I couldn't recall the last time I was in such a good mood. Even my hunts didn't clear my head like the news of my mother's death. I could only imagine the sheer glee I'd experience from dancing on her corpse.

For the entirety of the drive, I kept my attention fixed on the buildings and houses we zipped past. If I spoke, I realized, my contentment would show. Though I was finished dealing with my mother, I didn't want to let my mask slip, not even in the company of our everyday employees. For all the man in the driver's seat knew, I was silent with grief.

Now, that was laughable. I held back a derisive snort. Thinking I'd grieve that old bat for even a second was ridiculous.

I shook it all off. I didn't need to dwell on thoughts of my mother anymore. The bitch was gone, and soon, the worms would be feasting on her formaldehyde-infused carcass.

On arriving at a tall, sleek building on the outskirts of

downtown, I thanked my driver and advised him to stay nearby. Hopefully, this exchange wouldn't take long so I could get back to my glorious day.

My heels clicked against the polished marble floor as I made my way to an elevator around the corner from the reception desk. A large bank owned the building, and different businesses rented out each floor. There was a psychiatrist's office, a chiropractor, a couple of different realtors, the law firm our family used, and several others.

Since my father died three years earlier, I'd been in and out of this building plenty of times. Before that, we'd not dealt with many lawyers.

Well, not since my twin and I were younger anyway.

Recalling some of our close calls from ages ago tempered my good spirits, serving as a pointed reminder of where I was and why I was here.

Whenever we got into trouble, our parents never hesitated to use our family lawyers to brush the misdeeds under the rug.

Way back in tenth grade, one of the girls in my chemistry class attempted to bully me. Little did she know, though, that I didn't give a damn about anything a fifteen-year-old girl had to say. Plus, unlike me, her family wasn't wealthy or influential. They weren't poor, either, but her parents were doctors, not Fortune 500 executives like mine.

Regardless, the little bitch got on my nerves. One day, I snuck away from the cafeteria during lunch and broke into the chemistry lab. I stole a lye solution and used it to replace the girl's hand lotion.

As confident as I'd been that no one could catch me, I'd been spotted breaking into the chem lab on the school's security cameras. The girl's family wanted to press charges, but my parents put a quick end to their ideations of justice. I was kicked out of that ritzy little private school, but nothing stuck to my record.

Garrett'd had a couple of his own run-ins with irritating classmates, and he was booted from the same school less than six months after me. Honestly, I think he did it because he missed being near me.

Dealing with lawyers and hush money was the only time our mother and father would pay attention to us. Unless, of course, my mother was busy critiquing my appearance or reminding me of what a disappointment I was.

It doesn't matter anymore. She's dead. He's dead. They're both gone forever.

I smiled to myself as the elevator ground to a halt.

A bell chimed, and the doors slid open to reveal a floor-to-ceiling window with a view of the glittering skyscrapers of downtown Chicago. The entire place was all straight lines and modern design, the only splashes of color coming from a few abstract paintings on the dark-gray walls.

I made my way to an L-shaped desk, gave the receptionist my name, and took a seat to wait for the lawyer to come collect me. In the meantime, my twin emerged from the same elevator I'd just used. I could tell by the lightness in his stride he was experiencing the same sense of relief I was.

We waited in silence, the only sounds being the building's ventilation, the occasional incoming call, and the faint click of the receptionist's keyboard.

With each passing moment, anxiety began to build in my chest.

Where was Eddie? Shouldn't he have been here by now?

As I leaned over, preparing to ask Garrett about our older brother, a familiar, well-dressed man emerged from the hallway that wrapped behind the elevators. Aside from a few slivers of gray in his slicked back hair, little had changed about the lawyer over the past decade.

He beckoned us over. "Good afternoon, Darla, Garrett. I'm very sorry to hear about your mother. All of us here at the firm offer our heartfelt condolences."

I offered a smile I hoped was more wistful than impatient. His words were just as hollow as mine. "Thank you, Rupert. We'll be glad to get all the legalities out of the way so we can have time to grieve our loss."

"Of course. Let's head back to my office."

"Wait." My twin stood in place, gesturing at the empty waiting area. "Where's Eddie? Shouldn't we wait for him?"

The lawyer's expression could have been carved from marble for all the emotion it conveyed. "No need. He's already back in my office."

"Already back in your office?" I parroted the words before I could stop myself, biting down on my tongue to keep my surprise contained.

Why in the hell was Eddie already there? What had they been discussing while we'd been made to wait?

If the sharpness of my tone affected the lawyer, he didn't show it. "Come on. We'll discuss this in my office."

If this son of a bitch says "my office" one more time, I swear I'll put one of my crossbow bolts through his throat.

I clenched my jaw to keep my temper hidden. "After you, then."

The trek down the dim, carpeted hall was the longest of my life. My instincts were screaming at me, like a thousand voices in the back of my head, telling me something about this situation was wrong.

This was supposed to be simple. I'd ensured my Joan Crawford wannabe received the best medical care in her final days and brought my daughter to visit her every single godforsaken day since the stroke that had landed her in the hospital. Well, I missed one day, but surely that wouldn't be an issue. As long as I humored her, my portion of the inheritance—hundreds of millions of dollars, as well as a permanent stake in the family's tech business—was guaranteed.

That was our agreement, and I'd honored my end. She couldn't change her mind now. She was dead, for Chrissake.

Then why was Eddie talking to Rupert Taft before we got here? What were they scheming?

Stepping into Taft's corner office, I blinked at the sudden brightness of the sunlight filtering through the windows.

Eddie sat in one of the two armchairs in front of the lawyer's mahogany desk. His gaze oozed mistrust, just as I was sure mine did. Sweat beaded between my shoulder blades, though the air-conditioning in this building was set to frigid.

This was supposed to be simple.

No matter how many times I repeated the mantra to myself, it didn't change the way the incessant voices of doubt in the back of my head chorused that something was wrong.

Once the door was closed, Taft gestured to a love seat against the wall, facing his desk. "Have a seat. I'll try to make this as quick as I can so you can...get back to grieving."

Between the knowing glint in his eyes and his emphasis on the word *grieving*, I wanted to rush across the room and scalp him where he sat. Instead, I clenched both hands into fists and took a seat next to my twin.

Taft shuffled through a few papers. "I know you're all busy people, so I'll get right down to brass tacks. I have copies of the witnessed will for all of you to take home with you today, and I'll be setting up separate meetings with your spouses and children."

"With our...*what*?" I mentally cursed myself for letting the disbelief slip out.

Taft's cool gaze met mine for half a second before his attention returned to the papers. "With you and your brother's spouses, ma'am. Anyway, as I was saying, down to brass tacks. Your mother's liquid assets are to be split evenly between your daughter," he gestured at me, then to my twin, "your two children, and Eddie."

The floor seemed to fall out from beneath me, and his words were difficult to make out over the thunder of my pulse.

These are just the liquid assets, just the cash in her bank account. That means we've got to get something...the business! It turned record profits last year. If I have control of the business, I'll make more than Eddie's measly inheritance...

The lawyer flipped to another sheet of paper, and I fought desperately to anchor my drifting thoughts. "The funds for those who are underage will remain in a trust. A portion of that trust will be accessible at age eighteen to pay for college expenses, and the remainder will be released once the individual turns twenty-two or completes an undergraduate degree, whichever comes first."

I bit down on my tongue until I tasted iron. I didn't even want to spare a look at my twin. I already knew what I'd find on his face.

Fury. Murderous rage.

"Your parents' business will be left solely in Eddie's hands. As for you two," Taft's gaze flicked to me and my twin. "You're each granted a sum of one million dollars."

The lawyer's words were like a slap to my face—like my wretch of a mother had risen from the grave to backhand me one last time before she laughed her way to Hell.

Though I wanted nothing more than to let loose on

Eddie and the smug prick of a lawyer, I wasn't so sure I could stop myself once I started.

Clearing my throat, I clasped my hands in my lap, tightening my grip until my skin burned. "I'm sorry, Rupert. There must be some mistake. I've been personally tending to our mother's health ever since she was admitted to the hospital. This was according to her specific request, and she assured me that I'd receive my fair share of the inheritance when she passed. As long as...as long as I helped her."

"Hm." Taft glanced at Eddie and then back at the documents on his desk. "Well, I'm sorry to say this, ma'am, but I don't see anything here about that stipulation. Look, I'm just reading the will the way your mother wrote it. You can look over the document yourself, and you can even consult with your own personal attorney if you'd like. If you believe part of this has been unlawful, you have the option to contest it in a probate court. However, that's not my job. There's no further action that can be taken here and now."

Oh, but there is. I can send one of my bolts through your wrinkly throat and watch you gasp for air until you collapse on your desk.

I silenced the murderous thought. "You don't understand. My mother told me repeatedly that I'd receive my share of the inheritance. She didn't say anything about a...a million! That's nothing! You can't honestly think she left two of her children a pittance, can you? We're her flesh and blood!"

Unperturbed, Taft held out his hands. "This is the will your mother has on file. I'm just reading her final instructions."

The remainder of the meeting was a blur, even though there wasn't much else to address. And my fucking bozo of a twin didn't utter a single word. But he gave me a few side glances, implying he thought I was somehow to blame.

We rode back to my house in silence.

After each grabbing a bottled water from the fridge, we made our way back to my soundproofed shooting range. Practice wasn't my goal, not right now. We needed to have a discussion, and although there was no one in the house, I'd feel better inside the walls of my haven.

As soon as the door latched closed, he whirled around, his face a mask of fury. "You said that old bat was going to leave you almost everything! Most of Eddie's one-third of the inheritance plus the remaining assets would be shared between us. We'd control the company. What the fuck happened? What's this about one million? How didn't you see that coming?"

I knew that son of a bitch was going to try and pin the blame for this on me. Not today.

Taking a swift step forward, I jabbed an index finger against his chest. "How didn't I see that coming? Are you kidding me? I was the one forced to deal with her day in and day out while you...what? While you stalked a couple of FBI agents? While you came within an inch of being spotted at the scene of a murder? One of *our* murders?"

A flush crept onto his cheeks, and he shifted away from my advance. Though he had a solid seven inches of height and close to eighty pounds of muscle on me, I'd never once let him back me into a corner.

We were equals, and I wasn't about to let him forget that now.

I threw my hands up in the air. "You know how duplicitous that woman could be! Has she ever told us the truth about anything? Maybe you're right. Maybe I shouldn't have believed her, but what the hell else was I supposed to do?"

He held up a hand and patted the air. "I know, I know. I didn't mean to snap at you. It's her fault. Why in the hell would she leave the fortune to our sniveling little brats? And you know damn well neither Eddie nor any of them could ever run a tech company. And don't even get me started on our brother."

White-hot rage roiled in my chest, threatening to explode from my body like a volcano. As much as I tried to silence the anger, it wouldn't dissipate. "You're right. We need to deal with them. There's got to be something we can do to force them to hand over their inheritance to us. But we need to have a clear head. We need to...to let go of this shit, even if it's just temporary."

I shot my twin an expectant glance.

Understanding dawned on his face, and his stance relaxed. "We need to hunt."

"Yes. We need to hunt."

22

The daylight had turned a darker shade of gold, and it wouldn't be long until the sun started its slump below the horizon. All in all, I couldn't have asked for a better day for a hunt. The temperature hadn't climbed much higher than eighty, and a pleasant breeze still brushed through the trees, carrying with it the fresh scents of spring.

As my brother and I stalked across the gravel lot, I spared a glance at the sign at the entrance.

Welcome to Northern Cardinal Campground!

Mentally, I scoffed at the cheery intonation. I could still recall spotting that godforsaken sign from my seat in the back of a bus as we were jostled about by all the divots and bumps in the poorly maintained road. More than twenty-five years had passed since we'd first made the unpleasant journey from Chicago to Northern Cardinal Campground, but the memory was still seared into my brain like a brand.

Of all the places our parents could've sent us over the summer, I'd never understand why they selected a campground in the middle of rural Illinois. They'd both been born and raised in Chicago, and our family's business was built on technology. We were about as far from the average camper as any family could get.

And yet, rather than deal with us over the summer after we'd finished sixth grade, our parents had shipped us off. According to my mother, lots of families would've killed to get their children a spot at such a beautiful summer camp.

A faint howl drifted in through the partially open windows of my cabin, along with the quiet chatter of night birds and other woodland creatures. Three bunk beds lined either side of the room, and of the six girls, I was the only one still awake.

As backward as it seemed, the noises made by the animals nearby weren't what kept me from sleeping. I couldn't drift off because it was so quiet and still. The eerie atmosphere was unlike anything I'd experienced—in the city, something was always moving. Cars were always on the road, people were always working, life was always advancing.

Out here, there was...nothing.

Pulling my knees up to my chest, I tightened the blanket around my shoulders and squeezed my eyes closed. If I stayed in this position, I was bound to fall asleep eventually.

I clenched my jaw and shook off the memory, but as I reached for the passenger side door, I realized my brother's stare was similarly fixed on the welcome sign.

Sighing, he raked a hand through his hair. "Why'd we buy this place again?"

"So we could do this." I gestured to the woodland we'd just left in the direction of the woman and teenage girl we'd spent the afternoon stalking. "You have to admit, there's something sort of 'full circle' about coming back to this place."

"Maybe." Garrett gripped the steering wheel, his knuckles turning white. "I always figured we bought it as a 'fuck you' to mom and dad for forcing us to come here those two summers. I never really considered hunting here. Not until now anyway. But it seems a little too risky to me."

"Risky? This from the man who stalked a federal agent at one of our kill sites."

"Okay, I don't want to argue. But I suppose you're right. It is...*fitting*."

I didn't say the words out loud, but we both knew the reason the location was so fitting.

This hunt was personal.

We didn't know the woman and her niece. The pair had set up their tent and supplies near a small waterfall in the woods, and they'd spent the rest of the afternoon hiking... unaware my brother and I were shadowing their every move.

The girl was two years older than my daughter—though I'd have given just about anything to swap their places today. For now, our prey would have to serve as my daughter's surrogate.

My mother had always followed her own set of rules and morals, but this...this took the cake. That bitch had lied to my face, had held me hostage to her presence for the final weeks of her life, and had forced so many interactions between me, her, and my daughter that I'd lost count.

I'd tolerated it for the inheritance. But the old hag's motive escaped me.

Now? All that money I was supposed to receive, the money to which I was rightfully entitled, all of it would go to my good-for-nothing, spineless daughter while I was left with a pitiable sum that wouldn't maintain my current rate of spending for a single year.

Sliding into the passenger's seat, I clenched my hands into fists to keep the bout of rage to myself. I'd already had to hold Garrett back from following Eddie to his hotel. If I displayed my anger, chances were, he'd view it as permission to go marinate Eddie in the bathtub with a blow dryer.

No, that wouldn't do. With the contention in the lawyer's office yesterday, the cops would come right to our doorstep if Eddie was found dead. We couldn't touch him. Not yet. Not until we had a plan.

As much as I wished I could pull it off, I couldn't kill my daughter either.

I gritted my teeth and glanced back toward the woodland. The little brat camping with her aunt bore a slight physical resemblance to Karina, but the way she talked...her soft-spoken questions, the uncertainty oozing out of every pore...whoever had raised her had screwed her up just as badly as my husband had screwed up our kid.

Don't worry. I'll put the little bitch out of her misery tonight.

My brother turned the key over in the ignition, and I ripped my attention away from the woods. Now that we'd stashed our supplies in some bushes, we'd move the car to a less conspicuous location and make our way back on foot. If there were any bystanders—which there weren't, as we'd checked the area thoroughly—they'd believe we were long gone. The car was a rental that I'd paid for with a fake ID, and the make and model would never be traced back to either of us.

For nearly a decade, this routine had worked flawlessly.

Neither of us spoke as we coasted away from the parking lot. I caught a glimpse of the welcome sign in the rearview mirror, reminding me of the exact same sight twenty-six years ago.

"Oh my god, Laura. I can't believe she doesn't know what whittling is." Millie brushed a strand of blond hair from her face and rolled her eyes dramatically.

"Of course she doesn't. She doesn't know anything." The

redhead on the bench beside her, Laura, raised a small knife. "Okay, dummy. It's when you take a pocketknife...you know what that is, right?"

My stomach twisted itself in knots, my throat tightening as tears threatened the corners of my eyes. "Y-yes. I know what a pocketknife is." I was so out of my element, I didn't know how else to respond.

The camp counselors had broken us into groups, and the one I'd been assigned to work with that afternoon was filled with girls from small towns and farms. They'd been raised around the wilderness. They were familiar with this alien land I'd barely ever seen before this week. I'd heard the term "culture shock" used in television shows, and I figured this had to be it.

Not only did I have zero idea how anything worked in this wilderness, I'd also never been stuck somewhere no one knew my family's name. Even on my first day at private school, the importance of who my parents were had carried weight. The other students had known not to screw with me because my family was powerful.

But these girls? They didn't know, and they didn't care. None of them lived in Chicago. None of them cared about the tech industry, and none of their parents were seeking reelection on the city council—a position my family could make or break for them.

As Laura explained how to whittle a stick, Millie and two others looked on with a combination of pity and amusement.

I wished I could take the sharpened stick from Laura's hand and jab it into each girl's eyeballs. Nothing would've made me happier than their shrieks of terror as they clamped their hands over their eye sockets, blood and fluid oozing from between their fingers as their worlds went dark forever.

I blinked away the memory, and when I glanced at the rearview mirror again, the sign was gone. Laura and the other girls had done their best to make my life miserable that summer, but each time I found my anxiety rearing its ugly head, I simply pictured their mangled corpses or imagined the litany of ways I'd have loved to kill them.

Eventually, toward the end of the six-week summer camp, the group lost interest in picking on me. I suspected they'd grown bored because they could no longer elicit a reaction, but I couldn't be completely sure.

Garrett had it just as bad, if not worse than me. Girls were notorious for being emotionally cruel, but boys often trended toward physical abuse. Back then, my brother was still a scrawny little thing, barely taller than teenage me.

Laura's brother, James, on the other hand, was two years older than us. After he'd learned his sister was leading the charge to pick on the little rich kid from the city, he'd banded together with a few of his pals to make my brother's life miserable. For a beat, I'd been convinced he was going to lose his cool and slit James's throat while he slept.

"You want to know what I do?" My voice was barely above a whisper. We were sitting together on the edge of a dock while the other kids swam around at a nearby beach.

My brother gave me a curious look. "What?"

"I just imagine what it would be like if I'd stabbed them all in the eye. Or if I'd taken one of their pocketknives and carved the skins off their faces. Or if I'd held their heads underwater until the bubbles stopped."

Appearing intrigued, my brother leaned back and studied the swimming campers. "Or maybe what they'd look like if they drowned out there right now, and the cops found their bodies a week later. They'd be all swollen and gray, like we saw on that one website, remember?"

A smirk crept onto my face as I nodded. "Exactly. Doesn't that make you feel better?"

He grinned. "Yeah. It does."

More than twenty-five years later, as the memory played out in my head, the same smirk tugged at my lips.

"What?" He must've caught me smiling.

"Remember Laura and James McKinney?"

He chuckled. "Oh, I remember them, all right. I remember how Laura screamed when she saw her brother down in that creek bed."

"And how the blood from his head washed away in the water." I leaned back in my seat with a contented sigh. "They kept him on life support for almost five years after that."

My brother snorted. "Probably because they thought they'd have a better chance of getting Mom and Dad into a courtroom or something."

The smile on my lips didn't wane.

Nearly three decades ago, my twin and I had come into our own at Northern Cardinal Campground. Tonight, I'd kill that mousy little brat we'd stalked, and Garrett would slit her aunt's neck from ear to ear. With a fresh kill behind us, and our minds clear, we'd come up with a plan to do away with Eddie for good and claim our rightful fortune.

23

Rolling over to her side, Rose Seller tucked a hand beneath her pillow and squeezed her eyes closed a little tighter. As she brushed her fingertips against the hilt of her hunting knife, she was granted a small measure of relief. Her niece's breath was slow and rhythmic, leading Rose to believe the girl was fast asleep.

Good. At least one of us is getting some rest.

And at least they weren't staying at Northern Cardinal Campground after tonight. Goose bumps crept down Rose's back as she went through her memories of her and Sophie's hike that day.

The shadows Rose swore she'd spotted in the trees...the rustling of leaves she and Sophie had both caught on more than one occasion.

Rose was an experienced camper, hiker, and fisher, but she couldn't recall the last time she'd been that unnerved at a campsite in Illinois.

In Montana, where bears and mountain lions roamed freely? Sure, camping out there was nerve-racking, sometimes. But in Illinois?

She closed her hand around the grip of the hunting knife. For a beat, she wished the blade were a handgun or a rifle. Rose had never seen the sense in carrying a firearm to a campsite like Northern Cardinal, but tonight, she was second-guessing many of her convictions.

What do you really think is out there? There aren't any bears in this part of the country, and mountain lions are pretty rare. Besides, they're easy to scare off. You've done it before, for crying out loud. Just make yourself as big as possible and be really, really loud.

Usually, recalling the trip when she'd scared off a mountain lion and saved her and her sister's lives brought Rose a measure of contentment and pride. But as she recalled the eerie sensation of being watched all afternoon, the sentiment fell short.

With the end of her niece's school year around the corner, Rose had planned a camping trip for the two of them so they could celebrate a little early. Sophie was the oldest daughter of Rose's big sister, and the two of them had been close since Sophie was a baby. Sophie's sophomore year had been challenging, as teenage years often were. Since Sophie had always enjoyed the outdoors, Rose's hope was that a weekend away would be just the thing her niece needed to power through the remainder of the school year.

And now, the trip would end with Aunt Rose turning into a paranoid whacko.

Ha ha. It's not just me. Sophie felt like someone was watching her too.

Probably because Aunt Rose had made her paranoid.

They were fine. More than likely, other hikers were in the area, triggering the bizarre feeling of being watched.

This rationalization finally brought Rose a snippet of

relief. Her muscles relaxed, and her thoughts began to drift away from reality.

At some point, she must've fallen asleep.

But then, with a sharp breath, Rose snapped her eyes open as if she'd fallen into a vat of icy water. Her heart slammed against her chest with so much force, she worried the disturbance would wake Sophie.

Why was she so panicked?

She'd heard a noise.

As Rose glanced at her sleeping niece, the girl didn't move aside from the slow rise and fall of her chest. Her face the picture of serenity.

Okay, so there wasn't a noise. It was probably a nightmare.

Rose couldn't recall even the slightest detail from her dream, if she'd even had one.

Puzzling over what could've elicited such a visceral reaction from her sleeping body, Rose slumped forward and propped her arms on her knees.

I need to trust my instincts. If I'm wrong, Sophie will have a great story to use against me until my dying days. But if I'm right, something's out there.

Hairs on the back of Rose's neck stood at attention. She strained to listen for any—

Crack.

The disturbance was so slight, she doubted she'd have caught it if she hadn't been paying attention. A leaf, or perhaps a twig, followed by an even quieter rustle.

That'd sounded like...the swish of fabric.

There isn't something out there. Someone *is out there.*

Rose needed no more convincing. She and Sophie were getting the hell out of there.

With each movement slow and deliberate to avoid making any noise, Rose pushed away her sleeping bag and scooted closer to her niece. As she gently shook Sophie's shoulder, she prepared to clamp her other hand over the girl's mouth if she screamed.

Groaning softly, Sophie rolled onto her back and blinked up at Rose.

Rose rested an index finger over her lips. In the darkness of the tent, she just made out Sophie's expression of shock and confusion. To Rose's relief, her niece remained silent as she wiggled into a sitting position.

One hand still on Sophie's shoulder, Rose leaned closer to the teen. "Put on your shoes, fast. There's someone outside. We need to get to the truck so we can get out of here. We'll come back for our stuff later."

Sophie nodded, and the two of them pulled on their shoes as quickly and quietly as possible. Clamping her hand around the keys to keep them from jingling, Rose tucked them into her pocket and the hunting knife into the waistband of her sweatpants. She and Sophie each carried their cells, but at the moment, Rose wasn't sure what good calling the police would do.

What would they say? *"Help, there might be a person creeping around our campsite, but it also might be a dog or something, we don't really know. I'm just scared shitless, and I'm going to run for my life to be on the safe side."*

Reaching for the zipper at the front of their tent, Rose mentally cringed at the quiet separating of metal teeth as she opened the flap.

A rush of cool night air whispered in to greet her, and she paused before motioning for Sophie to follow her. Visibility outside was better than she'd imagined, thanks to the waning moon set high in the inky-black sky. The pale light would barely be visible once they were out of the clearing and into the trees, but Rose didn't dare retrieve a flashlight.

The beam would make them easy targets for whatever —*whoever*—was out there.

And Rose was certain someone was stalking their campsite.

Lush grass around their tent rendered her footsteps nearly silent—a relief for Rose, even though the clearing left them exposed. Only a small patch of woodland stood between them and Rose's truck. But to Rose and her paranoid state, they might as well have needed to cross Omaha Beach.

Turning back to Sophie, Rose pointed toward the trees. Understanding dawned in Sophie's expression, and though the poor girl's eyes were wild with fear, she nodded.

Good kid. You know where we're headed.

With Sophie right on her heels, Rose trotted into the thicket of trees.

She and her niece got five steps in before she realized what a terrible mistake she'd made.

In the blink of an eye, the massive oak in front of them seemed to explode to life. Moonlight glinted off the polished silver of a long blade as a hulking figure leapt out from behind the tree. Though Rose's attention snapped straight to the machete, she noted the assailant was clad from head to toe in black—a hooded sweatshirt, cargo pants, and boots.

As he arched his arm backward to prepare the first swing of the vicious blade, a million and one thoughts rushed through Rose's mind, but instinct took over.

Though Rose didn't remember unsheathing the hunting knife at her back, the blade somehow appeared in her hand as she observed the angle of the crazy man's slash. At the last second, she hopped backward to avoid a blow that would've cleaved her shoulder off her body. She bumped into Sophie behind her, but at least neither of them had gotten cut.

Unbothered by the miss, the man in black did something Rose hadn't anticipated.

He smiled. Not a cheery expression. Not even an expression of mocking derision.

His grin was laced with sheer malevolent glee.

Rose's stomach twisted as adrenaline surged through her body. She wasn't about to become a willing participant in this psycho's plans.

Raising the hunting knife, Rose dared a glance at Sophie. She was ghost-white. "Stay behind me."

Terror shook Sophie's voice. "O-okay."

"Oh, trust me, little girl. That won't save you." The bass in the man's growl rumbled like thunder, his tone oozing self-satisfaction.

He didn't wait for Rose or Sophie to respond before he charged forward to close the short distance between them. For a big guy, he moved like a cat.

As he slashed the machete in a diagonal downward arc, Rose pivoted on the balls of her feet. Air whooshed past her abdomen where the blade nearly disemboweled her, but before she could recover to try to land her own blow, the man used his remaining forward momentum to turn the machete around and swing lower.

Rose twisted to the side at the last moment, but pain seared along her hip, jolting through her nerves like a lightning bolt. A yelp of surprise slipped past her lips.

The maniacal grin on the man's face widened.

Blood pounded in Rose's ears as desperation began to claw at the back of her mind. She needed to land a hit, and she needed to do it soon if she and Sophie were to stand a chance.

She couldn't fail. If the guy overtook her, Sophie didn't have any way to defend herself.

Rose would not leave her defenseless. One way or another, Sophie *would* get out of these woods tonight.

Despite her injury, the desire to protect her niece sent a wave of renewed determination through Rose. Tightening her grasp on the hunting knife, she feigned a step toward the man in black, as if she'd suddenly decided to go on the offensive.

The fake worked. As the man lunged forward with his machete leading the way, Rose twisted backward and to the side. While the lunatic was still working to correct himself, she slashed the hunting knife in front of her, aiming for the side of his neck. At the last second, he brought his free arm up to block Rose's blow, but the fine blade still dug deep into his forearm.

Roaring in pain like a wounded boar, he backpedaled out of Rose's reach.

Though the warmth of blood dripped down her side, the adrenaline coursing through Rose's veins had numbed the pain of her injury. As far as she could tell, her wound was superficial.

She *hoped* it was superficial, but she didn't have time to assess the damage. She needed to keep this prick on the defensive until she either got the chance to land a killing strike or he scurried away with his tail between his legs.

The man glanced from his injured arm to Rose. "You bitch! You're going to pay for that!"

Though Rose expected him to raise his machete and charge forward, a flicker of movement in her periphery jerked her attention to a second shadowy figure.

"Aunt Rose! Watch out! There's someone else, and they have a—"

The girl's warning was cut short as a projectile shot through the air and slammed into Rose's shoulder blade. An explosion of pain spread downward into her side. The force of the blow set Rose off-balance, and if not for her niece rushing over to her, she'd have toppled forward.

No. You're not falling down, Rose Seller. Remember what Dad used to tell you and Jamie. What doesn't kill you makes you stronger!

Gritting her teeth against the pulsing pain, Rose took stock of her two adversaries. The man had backed away for the time being, his free hand clutching the deep wound in his arm. Though the second person was smaller and ostensibly less formidable than the man, they cradled a weapon in their arms, the same weapon that had fired at Rose.

What is that?

The person—a woman, Rose suddenly realized—advanced through a sliver of moonlight, revealing a state-of-the-art crossbow. Rose's father was an avid hunter, and he kept an entire collection of compound bows and crossbows. This was no high-powered rifle, but crossbows were brutal weapons in the right hands.

Raising the stock of the bow to her shoulder, the woman began to take aim.

"Shit!"

As if Sophie read her mind, the girl clamped a hand around Rose's uninjured arm and jerked her behind a tree just as a crossbow bolt whipped through the air.

"You think you can hide from me?" The woman with the crossbow guffawed. "After what you did to my brother? Not a chance, ladies."

Rose rested one hand on the rough bark of the tree, pausing to take in a deep breath of desperately needed air. As she inhaled, she was greeted with a sick, sucking sensation in her right side. Pain lanced outward from her ribs, tipping her off as to what had happened.

The crossbow bolt that struck her shoulder had pierced through the top of her rib cage. Her lung was collapsing. Warm blood crept up the back of her throat as she reached into her pocket for the truck keys.

"Aunt Rose?" Sophie's voice was hushed, almost lost under the crunching of leaves and dirt preceding the woman as she and her crossbow drew nearer.

Rose grabbed the girl's wrist and shoved the keys into her hand.

Sophie's eyes grew as wide as a pair of dinner plates, but as blood trickled from the corner of Rose's mouth, she must have read the desperation in her gaze.

Rose closed her niece's hand around the keys and gave it a squeeze. "Love you, kiddo."

Tears sprang to Sophie's eyes. "Love you, Auntie."

"Oh, how sweet." The woman dragged the final word out for several syllables. "We'll make sure you die together so your love can remain eternal. Isn't that poetic?"

Rose placed a hand on Sophie's shoulder before giving her a little push. "Go."

As Sophie sprinted out from behind the tree, Rose emerged right after her. Unsurprisingly, the woman's crossbow was trained on them.

However, the woman hesitated, seeming to calculate which of them posed the greater threat. Her crossbow wavered between aunt and niece, but the bolt didn't fly.

That moment of pause was exactly what Sophie needed. The teen took off.

Making her decision, and the woman turned her aim toward the teenager, but Rose dug deep in her energy reserves and charged toward her, the hunting knife leading the way.

Rose was greeted with a sense of grim satisfaction as her blade ripped into the woman's shoulder, slicing downward, slamming into her clavicle.

Before she could prepare for another swing, a rough hand took hold of her hair, ripping a fistful of it from her scalp. Rose blindly jabbed the knife backward at her assailant, his grunt of pain telling her she'd hit something.

"Enough of your shit." He yanked harder on her hair with a growl.

"Fuck you, asshole."

Cold metal pressed against Rose's throat, and in her last few seconds, she offered a prayer that her niece would make it away safely.

24

Sophie Hendrix hated running.

Her mom always liked to remind her that cardio was good for her heart, but anytime Sophie tried to run for exercise, she thought she'd rather die young than subject herself to this torture every day for the rest of her existence.

As she hurtled through the woods, branches whipping at her cheeks, none of the usual complaints rolled through her mind. A stitch bloomed in her side right away, but she didn't give a shit. Her aunt was back there fighting for her life, and unless she summoned some latent X-Men superpowers, the odds were against her. Aunt Rose's only hope was Sophie getting to the truck, driving the hell out of here, and getting them help.

Even then, the prospects were grim.

Sophie wasn't a fan of most of her high school classes, but she loved biology. Learning about how the human body worked was fascinating, but because of her studies, she was pointedly aware of the seriousness of her aunt's injuries. Maybe she could've convinced herself Aunt Rose was okay if it hadn't been for the blood on her lips, dripping down to her chin.

Terror sat like a block of ice in Sophie's chest, and no matter the sweat beading on her forehead, the constricted, freezing sensation wouldn't abate. Her back tingled and her scalp prickled as she imagined the attackers giving chase.

Sophie's breath came in labored gulps, the stitch in her side now stabbing at her like a javelin. Scurrying behind an old maple, Sophie pressed her back against the bark and gasped for air.

Had she outrun the two maniacs? Was she close to the truck? Or had she run in one big fucking circle?

Clamping her hand around the keys until the metal teeth bit into her palm, Sophie tried to take stock of her surroundings. A few slats of moonlight pierced through the leaves overhead, but that helped as much as someone shining a flashlight into a black hole.

Without relinquishing her grip on the keys, she dug into the back pocket of her jeans and pulled out her phone. When she unlocked the screen, her hopes sank to the ground as she noted the slash through the service bars.

The lack of cell service didn't make sense. Earlier in the day, she'd checked the weather forecast for the next few days. She'd had full service. Northern Cardinal Campground might have seemed like it was in the middle of nowhere, but there were cell towers everywhere these days.

Frustration mounted in Sophie's chest, nearly overtaking the worry for her aunt's welfare.

She had no service. She had no clue where she was. Even though the compass worked, panic was winning hard over that tool. How in the hell was she supposed to know which way to go—north or east or whatever—to get to the vehicle?

She could just continue to run straight, but what if she'd accidentally doubled back, and she was about to serve herself up to the two crazy people on a silver platter?

No. Don't be stupid. Aunt Rose didn't...didn't do that just so you could run back into their clutches like a directionally challenged moron.

Tears prickled the corners of her eyes as she recalled her aunt, and she bit her tongue to keep the despondency at bay.

Now wasn't the time. She needed to figure out which way she was headed, and—

Leaves rustled at her back.

Sophie's muscles went rigid, and she'd have stayed stone-still if it weren't for the keys digging into her hand.

The keys. The truck. Get out of here!

At least one of the lunatics had followed her. She didn't have to peek out from behind the tree—she was certain of it.

Think. You started running from the campsite. We followed a walking trail in. The campsite's south of where we parked, which means...

She patted the trunk of the tree, her heart skipping a beat as her palm met the soft growth of moss. Though moss didn't always grow on the north side of trees, the occurrence was frequent enough to have inspired an adage known by campers around the world.

If her back was against the north side of the tree, then she *was* headed in the right direction.

Another *crunch* turned her blood to ice water.

Which one of them was it? The woman with the deadly crossbow or the injured man with the machete?

Sophie didn't have time to figure it out. She needed to run. Her aunt had landed a blow to the woman as Sophie was fleeing the site, so she had to hope the injury would work to her advantage.

I'm getting out of here. I'm going to make sure these assholes pay for what they did.

She'd already hidden behind this tree for too long. If the woman didn't know she was here already, she would soon. Sophie had to act.

Straight. Keep going straight. You'll be at the truck soon.

With another deep breath, Sophie darted forward. As she sprinted out from behind the relative safety of the tree, a series of footsteps sounded not far from where she'd been hidden. Glancing over her shoulder, Sophie confirmed her stalker was the smaller of the two psychopaths—the woman with the crossbow.

Rather than run in a straight line, Sophie staggered her steps to zigzag. A few to the right, then one to the left, one to the right, three to the left. She didn't maintain any sort of discernable pattern. The key to evading enemy fire while running was to be unpredictable.

If she survived this, she could tell her mom that playing video games hadn't been a waste of time after all.

As Sophie neared a fallen log, she caught her first glimpse of a gravel clearing beyond the trees. Her spirits soared at the first sign of hope since this entire twisted debacle had begun. All she needed to do was make it to the parking lot, then she could get in her aunt's truck and drive the hell out of there.

Hopping over the log, Sophie tightened her grasp on the keys to reassure herself they were still there. As soon as she landed on the other side, a faint *twang* vibrated at her back. In the next instant, red-hot pain rushed up her leg as a crossbow bolt tore through her calf with a sickening wet rip.

Sophie cried out. By sheer willpower alone, she stopped

herself from pitching headfirst onto the ground. Though her muscles instantly cramped, a rush of adrenaline prevented the sensation overwhelming her. All she could do was hope the bolt had missed any major blood vessels.

Over the next few steps, her run devolved into a partial limp, but she wasn't about to give up. Not when she was so close.

Two steps to the right...

Whoosh.

A projectile whipped past her, and the woman cursed.

Based on the volume of her words, Sophie guessed she had a fair amount of distance on her. She'd been counting on the man's and woman's wounds to slow them down, but now that Sophie was wounded, too, she had to dig deep to make the final push to the parking lot.

Summoning a burst of speed she didn't even realize was possible, Sophie used the few moments after the missed shot to cover as much ground as she could.

Her sneakers crunched against the gravel as she sprinted out into the parking lot, nearly colliding with the passenger's side of her aunt's truck. Launching herself around the rear fender to the other side, Sophie pressed the button on the key fob to unlock the doors.

Time slowed to a crawl as she flung open the driver's side door and crawled inside. Her injured leg weighed too much as blood began soaking into her sock. Searing pain coupled with her calf muscle cramping worse than any charley horse she'd experienced in gym class made the leg useless.

Pain and fear clouded her thinking. Just because she'd made it inside the truck didn't mean she was safe. No doubt, a crossbow bolt could shatter the vehicle's windows.

Fumbling with the controls on the driver's door, she

managed to hit the lock. As she finally relinquished her grasp on the keys, her hands trembled so badly she was certain she would drop them.

Come on, come on. Focus. Just start the stupid truck!

Pulling in a deep breath, she firmly grasped the key between her thumb and forefinger, jammed it into the ignition, and turned the engine over. Part of her expected a horror movie cliché—for the engine to sputter and die—but her fears were allayed as the vehicle rumbled to life.

She threw the gearshift into drive and nudged the gas pedal. The fear free-falling through her brain wanted her to put the pedal to the floor, but after all her aunt had done for her, she wouldn't let this end with her crashing into a tree. And no way was she turning the headlights on, not just yet.

Prepared for a crossbow bolt to shatter the rear window at any point, Sophie eased the truck along the gravel path leading out of the campground. The road was winding, and even when she hit the headlights, the pitch blackness of the woods seemed to ooze in through the windows.

God, she hoped she wasn't going in a circle. The path had been straightforward in the daylight, but now she had no earthly idea where she was. All she could do was keep going and hope she came across a paved road.

She'd only driven for a few minutes, but to Sophie, it felt as if she'd been navigating these damn woods for hours. Her hands ached from her death grip on the steering wheel. The injury in her leg throbbed with every beat of her heart.

The twin beams of the headlights lit up a gentle curve ahead, and Sophie did her best to ignore the sense of impending doom that had followed her away from the campsite. Sadness prodded at her heart anytime her thoughts drifted to her aunt, but she didn't let herself dwell on the subject. She'd have time to process everything when she got to safety.

As she came around the bend, the lights shining on where the tree line abruptly ended, a renewed surge of hope and determination flooded her system.

She had no idea how close or far the two lunatics were, or if they'd hurried back to their own vehicle to give chase. Either way, it didn't matter.

Dead ahead of her was the smooth, dark pavement of the state highway.

25

As Amelia's cell buzzed against her nightstand, she jolted awake. Next to her, Zane groaned and rolled over to his side, though Amelia knew him well enough to realize he was just as awake as she. Rubbing the sleep from her eyes, she pushed herself to sit and grabbed the phone.

Sure enough, the caller was none other than her very own case partner, Dean Steelman.

As she swiped the screen, fatigue muzzled any attempts at a witty greeting. "Storm speaking."

"Morning, partner." Dean's voice carried the thickness of recent sleep. "Sorry to wake you, but this is important."

A hint of anticipation drove some of the cobwebs from her brain. "Lay it on me."

"The Kankakee County Sheriff's Office just called me. They've got a sixteen-year-old girl at the Kankakee hospital. She called the police once she reached the relative safety of a gas station after she was shot in the leg...with a crossbow."

Now Amelia fully woke up. "Where'd it happen?"

"Sheriff says the girl was camping with her aunt, and they were attacked in the middle of the night by a man with a machete. Then a woman showed up with a crossbow. The aunt held them off while the girl ran to their vehicle, and she drove to the closest town for help."

Amelia spat out a handful of four-letter words. "All right. Kankakee is about an hour and a half away. I'll meet you at the office in thirty?"

"See you there."

As Amelia rushed through an abridged version of her morning routine, Zane rolled out of bed and brewed a pot of coffee. In that moment, she'd never loved another human being more. At nearly four in the morning, she doubted any drive-through cafés were open on her route to work.

With a thermos and her messenger bag in hand, Amelia gave Zane a tight hug before hurrying out to her car. True to her word, she arrived at the FBI field office thirty minutes after their phone call.

According to Dean, Layton Redker had also received notification of the incident, so he was on his way to the field office too. But he'd stay behind in Chicago to "hold down the fort," as Dean put it.

Amelia and Dean wasted no time hopping into a black SUV, Amelia pulling out her work tablet to do some impromptu research while they drove. By the time they neared the edge of the city, she had a rough picture of the victim's background.

"Okay, so." Amelia blinked repeatedly as she glanced away from the bright tablet screen for the first time in almost twenty minutes. "Sophie Hendrix is sixteen, and she was camping with her aunt, Rose Seller, who's thirty-nine. Rose's sister, Jamie Hendrix, is Sophie's mother. Jamie and her husband, Pete Hendrix, were out of town visiting a friend this weekend."

Dean's eyebrows creased. "How'd you find all that? Social media?"

"Yep." Amelia always turned to social media as one of the first resources in establishing a person's background. "Sophie posted a picture of her and her aunt beside the welcome sign at Northern Cardinal Campground, which is where they were staying. According to her post, they were just planning to go hiking and get a feel for the place so they could come back to go fishing over the summer."

"Good plan. Makes sense. Did she post anything about running into other campers? Or post any pictures with other people in them?"

"Nothing that I saw, no. We'll have to ask her if she and Rose came across any people while they were there." Amelia paused, focusing on a niggling in the back of her head, part of her brain insisting something about Rose and Sophie was different. "You know, this is really bizarre. I mean, these perps have targeted pairs of campers for the past decade and only one other victim was a teenager."

With his focus glued to the road, Dean nodded. "Right. Six years ago, a seventeen-year-old. He was camping with his older brother."

"Something about this one seems...odd. None of the previous victims got away, obviously, but this is also really soon after the last murder. Sooner than we even discussed. Whatever the external stressor is that's driving them to escalate like this, I think it's getting worse."

Dean drummed his fingers against the wheel. "You're picking up on this serial killer thing pretty quickly." The sincerity of his compliment radiated in his smile while his eyes never left the road.

"Thanks. I suppose that's a good thing, being able to get

into the minds of these people. Any chance this is a copycat?"

So far, the FBI had carefully chosen which details they'd revealed to the public. The Fehu rune specifically had been kept under wraps, which Amelia appreciated. That little tidbit could have wound up in headlines across the country. And if she'd wondered whether these killers might've left other bodies without the symbol, complicating any connection to their case, copycats would muddy the waters even more. They couldn't afford that.

"I don't know, but I doubt it. Most of the coverage in the media has been local, and the story hasn't really picked up much national notice. Usually, when we see copycats, it's a crime that receives a lot of attention."

"So what do you think? How could someone get away from them for the first time in almost ten years?"

"That's a thing about serials. Something that's unique to them, for the most part." He glanced at her and lifted a shoulder.

"Eventually, after they get away with killing for so long, they start to think they're invincible." Amelia sensed it happening. The unsubs were slipping up, just as she knew they would.

"Right, and they think they can't be caught. Contract killers are like that too. Well, some of them. Is that what you think happened with Sophie?"

"The perps are escalating and getting more brazen because they think no one's going to catch them. So they have that feeling of invincibility, and then you couple that with them underestimating their victims." The more Amelia reasoned through the situation, the more sense it made.

"We can get Redker's opinion on it, too, but yeah, I think

that's the long and short of it. I doubt either of the killers thought a sixteen-year-old kid could get away from them. I mean, think about it. They've killed grown-ass men probably twice the size of Sophie Hendrix. Ron Dawson, for instance. He worked construction, and his license said he was six-four and two-eighty. If they could take him out, why would they think any differently about a high school sophomore?"

Serial killers were certainly a different breed, but Amelia reminded herself they could fall prey to common emotions like stress. Except, for a serial killer, stress manifested in a much different way.

Rather than pour themselves a stiff drink at the end of a rough workday or strap on a pair of running shoes, a serial killer was likely to return to the comfort or even the high they derived from killing.

What's happening in the lives of these two killers to lead them to escalating so fast? A divorce? Job loss? Or perhaps the death of someone they were close to? Not that someone capable of murdering thirty-nine innocent people would give a shit if someone passed away, but the experience could still prove stressful.

Amelia turned back to the tablet, preferring not to understand the inner workings of serial killers. As long as she understood their outer workings—as long as she could use that knowledge to catch them—she'd be satisfied.

Leave the dark depths of their psyches to folks like Layton Redker.

"What does Sophie Hendrix's statement look like so far?" Dean's question sent Amelia flipping through her many open program windows.

"There's not much of one yet. She's at Kankakee General Hospital. The crossbow bolt went through her calf, according to the notes here. It's a nasty wound, but so far it seems like she'll be okay. Her aunt, though..." A phantom hand squeezed Amelia's heart as she scanned the sheriff's notes. "According to Sophie, her aunt stayed behind in the woods, and she'd been struck more than once. The sheriff's department is conducting a search."

"All right, that's good. So when we get there, do you think we should split up? One of us go to the crime scene and the other go interview Sophie?"

Dean's tone was hopeful, even though Amelia couldn't honestly tell which role he'd prefer. "That sounds good. I'll, uh...take the crime scene?"

She figured she'd guessed right when he chuckled. "Works for me. This is something that's time sensitive, so I think it makes the most sense for us to divide and conquer, you know?"

He had a point. With each passing minute, the trail of the two killers grew colder.

26

For the first time, my brother and I fled the site of a murder we'd committed without killing both parties. Though I'd done my best to land a shot on the tires of the truck as that little brat drove away, I'd failed. We wanted to chase her, but ultimately, we cut our losses and started a winding path northward back to Chicago.

Even now, almost an hour and who knew how many miles later, I could still picture the fading red glow of those damn taillights.

Garrett gave me a look, jerked the car, and veered onto the shoulder of the road.

I already knew what he would say. He blamed me for missing the little bitch. For ruining our opportunity to silence her for good.

How much of our faces had she truly seen? The woods were dark at night, but surely she must've caught a glimpse of something. If nothing else, she'd heard us speak. Though at least we weren't stupid enough to use one another's names.

Ten years. Nineteen successful hunts, with only a couple

of close calls. And all of it was about to come to an end because some sniveling little teenager was adept at running serpentine?

My stomach dropped, and I gritted my teeth as I shoved open the driver's side door and stepped onto the uneven gravel.

Garrett was out of the driver's seat in an instant, kicking the door closed. He was in my face before I'd even shut my door. He jerked a thumb back at the car in the gravel pull-off. "What the hell happened with you?"

I went to hold my arms out at my sides, but instantly regretted the action. The majority of our drive had been spent pressing extra clothing to our injuries to stem the blood flow as well as we could.

Our wounds were too deep to attend to ourselves, but if we wanted to visit an emergency room, we'd need to come up with a story.

Would the medical staff even believe us? My brother had mentioned something about trying to play the sympathy card—we'd just lost our mother, after all. Wouldn't two distraught siblings make poor decisions in the aftermath of such a significant loss?

We could tell the nurses we'd been out late and were accosted by a hooded man as we were returning to our car. Or I could tell them my brother saved me when some drunk asshole put his hands where they didn't belong as we were leaving a bar. There was no shortage of tall tales we could concoct. We just had to make sure our versions were consistent, and I was having a hell of a time concentrating while I bled all over the place.

Would we have to file a police report? I didn't know how that shit worked.

For the first time in my life, I wished my parents were there to take care of this little problem.

I shook off all my questions and turned my attention back to my brother's intense stare. Aside from a sliver of moonlight piercing through a thin layer of clouds, the interior light of our car was the only source of illumination. One of us hadn't closed our door all the way.

Incompetence all night long.

Gritting my teeth against the pain in my shoulder, I pointed at my brother with my uninjured arm. "Don't tell me you're blaming me for this. Maybe *you* ought to tell *me* what happened. You're the one who couldn't land a hit on that woman! How'd you let her get the upper hand on you like that?"

He scoffed, shoving his fingers through his hair. "She didn't get the upper hand on me. She's dead!"

"Yeah, she's dead, and the Feds are going to find her fucking body!" I could hardly keep my ire in check. If my brother thought he was going to pin the blame for this debacle on me, I'd show him how wrong he was. "If you'd just killed her in the first place, then the girl wouldn't have gotten away, and we wouldn't be in this mess."

"Okay, okay." He held up his hands, wincing at the movement of his injured arm. "Listen, how was I supposed to know that bitch was Neo from *The Matrix*? Maybe we should've done a better job at picking our targets. Do you remember Tennessee? How we both almost died because we didn't realize that guy had a gun on him? It's the same principle."

I clenched my teeth together so hard I thought for a moment one of them might break.

He had a point.

Our recon had been sloppy. Usually, our targets were

naive college-aged kids with little-to-no wilderness experience. We made sure of that—we'd shadow them for an entire day, listening to their conversations, learning more and more about them.

With Sophie Hendrix and Rose Seller, we'd only stalked them for a few hours during the afternoon. Neither of them mentioned how much time they'd spent in the wilderness, nor did they bring up any self-defense training.

I'd assumed that meant we were in the clear. *But you know what they say about assuming.*

"All right." I couldn't continue to blame my brother for our mistakes. Not when it was clear we were both at fault. "We made a mistake. Both of us, and we let that little bitch get away. We can still fix this."

To my relief, my brother's posture relaxed as he lowered his hands. "We can. But we need to do it sooner than later."

He was right. "True."

"We don't know how much of our faces she saw. Shit, she could be with the cops right now, talking to one of those sketch artists."

I held up a hand before he could wade any farther into the deep end. "She didn't see us. Not well enough to work with a sketch artist. It was too dark for her to make out anything worthwhile. Nothing that'll put the Feds on our asses right away, at least. If we can take her out, we should be in the clear."

"Yeah, we should." Garrett bumped a toe against the car's bumper, thoughtful. "There shouldn't be anything at the scene that can tie them back to us. There's the crossbow bolt, but it's not like a bullet. It can't be traced back to a particular bow."

"We were wearing gloves, so there aren't any prints. And there wasn't anyone else at the campground." I didn't mention the small fact that we owned the fucking place. My brother wasn't an idiot, and I was certain he'd come to the realization already.

"Do you think the Feds have been interviewing the owners of all the other places we've hunted?"

Now I knew for sure it was on his radar. "I doubt it. They might call us, but that won't be enough to put us on the list of suspects."

"Then we're back to the girl. We know her and her aunt's names. That'll be enough to dig up some info on her, but it brings us back to the question of how we find her." He motioned to the driver's side. "Come on. We need to get back to the city so we can have these injuries taken care of. I'll keep driving the rest of the way."

Another wave of relief rolled over me. No matter what happened, no matter who slipped up during our hunts, we were still a team. As he circled around the front of the car, I dropped into the passenger seat. "She's more than likely in a hospital. I hit her in the leg when she was running, and I think it went clean through. That's going to be a substantial wound, and she'll have to have it treated."

Garrett pulled the driver's side door closed as he slid his muscled bulk behind the wheel. "So what do you want to do next? Go finish her off at the podunk hospital?"

"No. We need to get home and treat our injuries. Establish our alibis. Then we'll regroup and decide what to do with the girl."

My brother and I had never let any of our prey escape, but this was merely an intermission before the final act. I'd see to it my next bolt didn't miss.

27

Despite having rolled out of bed before four o'clock in the morning, Dean was wide awake by the time he arrived at Kankakee General Hospital. Compared to the hospitals in Chicago, the concrete building was the size of a shoebox.

How easily could the killers from the campground find their lone surviving witness in such a small space? That was, if they tried to come back for her at all.

We don't even know what she saw. Maybe they've already decided it isn't worth the risk.

In Chicago, at least, they had the option to transfer victims to different hospitals. Sophie Hendrix was a Chicago native, but until her parents returned to Illinois from their trip, the girl would remain in Kankakee. A U.S. marshal had already been notified, and soon, Sophie would have the closest thing she could get to a guardian angel.

As the automatic doors hissed open, Dean retrieved his badge. After providing his identification to a young man behind the reception desk, he followed the guy's directions to a room on the third floor. His dress shoes clicked along the tile, and during his trek, he only spotted two other people.

Well, at least they had that going for them. The fewer people who knew about Sophie's presence there, the better.

A pair of officers stationed near a corner room both turned toward Dean. Their stances stiffened as they took stock of the newcomer, and Dean couldn't blame them. His suit and tie were out of place in the small hospital.

With a smile he hoped was friendly and not tired, Dean held up his badge. "Good morning, Officers. I'm Special Agent Dean Steelman with the FBI. I'm here to speak with Sophie Hendrix. She's a witness in a case."

To Dean's relief, the pair visibly relaxed at the introduction.

"Nice to meet you, Agent Steelman. I'm Officer Landry." The taller of the pair stepped to the side and gestured at the closed door. "You can go on in. She was awake last I saw, poor kid." Genuine sympathy softened his weathered face. "Chief told us you and a marshal were on your way. Doc is done with her for now, so you can go in."

"Thank you. I appreciate it." Dean's gratitude was genuine. Not all cops were thrilled to work with the Bureau, but the pair at Sophie Hendrix's door were accommodating and helpful.

Officer Landry gave him a warm smile in response. "Let us know if you need anything."

After another thank-you, Dean braced himself as he reached for the door lever. All he knew about Sophie Hendrix, aside from what Amelia had learned from her social media search, was that she and her aunt were attacked by two unknown assailants at Northern Cardinal Campground, and she'd escaped with an injury.

The Kankakee County Sheriff's Department had already secured the crime scene, and Amelia was on her way to meet with them. Though Sophie had escaped, her aunt, Rose Seller, hadn't been so fortunate. The doctors had broken the news to Sophie when she refused treatment until she was informed. Although she'd been devastated, she'd also revealed she'd suspected her aunt hadn't made it.

Knocking lightly, Dean let himself into the dim room. The faint glow of the rising sun pushed through the half-closed blinds of the only window in the small space, and the recessed lights overhead had been turned off.

A pair of wide, fearful eyes settled on him as he stepped over the threshold. Sophie's dark-brown hair was pulled away from her pale face in a messy bun, and she sported a blue hospital gown. Her clothes had been bagged as evidence and sent to the FBI's lab in Chicago. A white bandage covered most of her left calf and shin, where she'd been hit by one of the killer's crossbow bolts.

She was lucky to be alive.

Badge in hand, Dean closed the door behind him. "Morning, Sophie. I'm Special Agent Dean Steelman with the FBI. I'm sorry for everything you're going through, but I need to ask you a few questions about what happened to you and your aunt."

Sophie's gaze remained glued to Dean as she pushed herself to sit up straighter. "Yeah, okay. The nurse told me the FBI were on their way. Does this mean..." She scrunched her nose. "Why is the FBI here and not just the cops?"

Dean pulled a chair up beside the hospital bed and took a seat. Though Sophie's eyes were bloodshot in a face as white as a sheet, her tone remained steady. Rather than a frightened child, she held herself like a young woman who wanted answers, and Dean couldn't help but admire her spirit.

When he pulled out his notebook, he also brought out his phone, placing the device on the bed beside her. "I'm going to take notes, but to be extra sure that I don't miss anything, mind if I record our conversation?"

She nodded. "Sure."

After he turned on the recorder and stated the date, time, and people present, Dean gave Sophie a small smile. "This case is in the FBI's jurisdiction because you and your aunt aren't the first folks these people have attacked. There's only so much I can reveal about the other cases, but suffice it to say, these people are very dangerous. They've hurt others."

Sophie swallowed and reached for the cream-colored blanket at her side. "They...they have? My aunt and I weren't the...first?"

"No, I'm afraid not. As far as we know, you're the first person who's survived one of these attacks. That makes anything you can remember very important. Even if you think it's a small, insignificant detail, it could still help. Do you think you could walk me through what happened?"

The girl's jaw tightened as she swiped at her glassy eyes. "Yeah, I can."

Scribbling notes periodically, Dean remained mostly silent while Sophie related her terrifying night in the woods. He refrained from asking too many questions to avoid potentially biasing her account of events.

As Sophie finished by recounting her desperate drive out of the campground, Dean was convinced she'd gone through hell and lived to talk about it.

Even after a decade in the FBI's Violent Crime Unit, Dean had to admit there was something especially unnerving about a pair of killers who stalked their victims in the woods in the dead of night.

"They're hunting prey."

Layton Redker's assessment echoed in his head.

Returning his attention to Sophie, he jotted down one last note. "Thank you. That was very helpful. I have a few follow-up questions for you now. Would that be all right?"

Sophie fiddled with the blanket on her lap but nodded. "Yeah, okay."

"Did you see anyone following you during the day? Notice anyone near your campsite?"

"We ran into a few people while we were hiking, but I don't think it was them. I did tell my Aunt Rose I felt like we were being watched."

"Really? Tell me more about that."

She smoothed the sheet folded over the blanket. "I don't know. At the time, it seemed silly. My aunt and I even joked about it. But we also kept checking our surroundings."

After a pause, Dean prodded for more. "And?"

"I'm sorry. We didn't see anyone following us."

"That's okay. This is all very helpful. Now, you said the attackers were a man and a woman, correct?"

Another nod. "Right."

"Were they wearing masks of any kind? Hoods or anything else to conceal their faces?"

The girl pressed her lips together. "I...no, I don't think so. But it was dark, so I didn't really get a good look at their faces. I mean, the moon was out a little bit, but not enough for me to really see what they looked like, you know? And I was standing behind my aunt. I might recognize them again, but I...I'm not sure. I'm sorry."

Dean held up a hand. "There's nothing to be sorry for. You didn't mention if they talked much. Did they?'

"Not really. They..." Her expression brightened, and he almost saw the lightbulb springing alive in her mind. "They didn't talk much, but one of them did say the other one was her brother. When she was talking to my...my aunt, she said she was going to make us pay for what she did to her brother."

Layton's profile sounded out in Dean's head for the second time. The BAU agent had concluded the killers were close, possibly either lovers or relatives.

"You said your aunt fought back. She had a knife?"

"She did, yeah."

"When she hit them, did you see where the injuries were?"

Though grim, her expression was determined. "I think so. She hit the guy first, and it looked like she was trying to aim for his throat, but he raised his arm at the last second. She got him right here," she held up her arm and made a slashing motion along the back of her forearm. "On his left arm. She didn't hit the woman until I was running away, though. I kind of looked back, but...I...I don't know." Tears sprang to her eyes. "I think she hit her shoulder, maybe?"

Dean pulled a few tissues from a box and handed them to the girl. "And they didn't try to chase you as you ran to your aunt's vehicle?"

Sophie blew her nose, and as she did, her energy seeped out of her now that the story was finished. "No. The woman wasn't running but she was following me. She used the crossbow to try to kill me, but she hit me in the leg. The bolt went straight through. The doctors said I'll have a scar, but it'll heal."

At least the poor kid hadn't been maimed and left with a lifelong disability by the same psychopaths who'd killed her aunt.

Knowing they were on the hunt for a brother and sister team who'd both sustained specific injuries was a tremendous step in the right direction compared to just an hour ago. But by itself, it wasn't enough.

As Dean wrapped up his interview with Sophie Hendrix, he vowed to make her aunt's heroic sacrifice count.

28

For the second time in less than a week, Amelia was grateful she'd worn boots as she accompanied the CSU at Northern Cardinal Campground. Now that the sun had climbed higher over the horizon, they could turn off their battery-powered work lamps and flashlights. Birds chirped in the trees alongside the chatter of squirrels and other wildlife Amelia couldn't identify.

Fortunately, there'd been no time for the area's scavengers to get to the crime scene yet. Sophie Hendrix had fled the area in her aunt's truck to call for help, and the sheriff's department had promptly come out to the scene. They'd investigated enough to locate Rose Seller's body and confirm the two perps were nowhere to be found.

After roping off the area around Rose and Sophie's campsite, they'd held the perimeter until the CSU arrived. The drive to Kankakee County from Chicago was only an hour and a half, so Amelia hadn't been terribly behind the curve when she'd arrived.

In the company of a sheriff's deputy, she made her way

through the tall trees to the clearing where Rose and her niece had set up camp.

Evidence collection tables had already been erected, along with numerous markers scattered throughout the clearing. The place was a hive of activity. Amelia turned to her crime scene-tech escort, a young woman with the state police named Erin Callahan. "What've you got so far?"

Without hesitation, Erin gestured to a slate-gray tent. "Here, let's start with the tent. The front flap is unzipped, so the vics must've exited there."

"No cuts?"

Erin shook her head, sending her auburn curls bouncing around her ears. "No. None."

For all the previous cases where a tent was found, there had been clear exterior slashes in the fabric. In addition, some of the victims were so panicked, they'd cut their way out of the tent instead of using the zipper.

Amelia mentally ran through her phone call with Dean, in which he'd summarized Sophie Hendrix's account of events. According to the girl, her aunt had woken her in the middle of the night after hearing a disturbance outside the tent.

Erin Callahan gestured to a handful of evidence markers near the tent. "One of my colleagues specializes in tracking human and animal prints. He's helping the techs examine the area around the body right now, but everything up until there is marked."

Callahan went on to explain which sets of tracks they believed were Rose's and Sophie's, as well as the tracks that likely belonged to the killers. Though Amelia had wondered about the numerous inconsistencies, listening to the tech relay virtually the same information as Deputy Foveaux at

Lake Henrietta was enough to put any lingering doubts to rest.

"One set of prints is much larger than the other." The crime scene tech hunched down beside a yellow evidence marker. "This is one of them, probably the highest quality. We'll be taking a plaster cast of it soon so your lab can compare it with what you've found at the other scenes."

Amelia already knew it would be consistent. She'd entertained the idea of a copycat killer for all of two seconds, but with every new tidbit of information, she was more and more certain this was the work of the same pair from the nineteen previous double murders.

Following Callahan into the woods, Amelia snapped photos of the area. The CSU had undoubtedly filled half a hard drive with their own pictures, but the camera gave Amelia a sense of purpose.

As she tailed Callahan, they were greeted by the voices of a few more crime scene techs, a sheriff's deputy, and a man in a dark jacket with *CORONER* on the back. Camera in hand, Amelia introduced herself.

One of the techs, Grant Holland—a tall, lanky fellow with a crop of black hair—gestured toward an evidence marker on the ground beside a tall maple. "Good timing, Agent Storm. We just finished photographing this."

Stepping carefully, Amelia made her way toward the tree. Though she didn't know what exactly they'd found, as she drew closer, dark splotches on the bark and dirt became more distinct. "Is that blood?"

"It is." Grant held up a plastic card, an item Amelia vaguely recognized. In addition to the well-known phenolphthalein strips to test for the presence of blood, the little plastic cards were used to differentiate human and animal blood. "We tested it, and it's human."

Amelia glanced over at the gurney positioned near the coroner. "Is it from the victim?"

Tucking the plastic test into an evidence bag, Grant shrugged. "It might be." He gestured toward a broad-shouldered deputy. "Deputy Gray is our tracking expert. What do you make of the tracks around that tree, Deputy?"

Gray took a few steps closer to the maple, his gaze glued to the ground. "There was definitely a scuffle here, but it's hard to say exactly who did what. We measured the victim's feet, and since her footprints are a different size than the others, I'm pretty confident I can tell which are hers."

Nearby, the coroner looked up from zipping up the body bag, showing an interest in the conversation.

"There are her prints, along with another set." Gray waved a hand at the tree. "They're similar in size, but slightly smaller. Whoever that person is, it appears they had an altercation with the victim right next to this tree. The blood could be from either of them, although…"

As he glanced at the coroner, Wade Dunlap, Amelia did the same. She was glad to see from his badge he was a trained field investigator, and an MD on top of that.

Absentmindedly readjusting his baseball cap, Dunlap cleared his throat. "Based on the injuries the victim sustained, it's possible the blood could be hers."

The deputy nodded. "All the samples are being sent to the FBI's lab."

"All right, good." As intriguing as the scene near the maple was, Amelia's curiosity drove the next question. "Can you give me a rundown of the injuries the victim sustained before she died?"

"Sure." The coroner beckoned Amelia over to the gurney. "The vic is Rose Seller, age thirty-nine. Based on the air temp, liver temp, and the time the relative reported the crime, I feel confident saying time of death was between two and three a.m. today. Cause of death appears to be a deep laceration along her throat that severed the carotid artery."

Dunlap paused and pointed at the dark splotch staining the ground. Like everything else, the site was littered with numbered evidence markers. Thin rays of sunlight shined through the leaves of the trees, illuminating the dark pool of blood and brightening its red tinge.

Amelia scanned the area near the blood, noting a handful of footprints next to the evidence markers.

The site of Rose Seller's final struggle.

Swallowing a sudden rush of anger at the psychopaths who'd preyed on Rose and her niece, Amelia turned back to the coroner. "All right. What about other injuries? Defensive wounds, anything along those lines."

Dunlap unzipped the black bag, revealing pale, blood-spattered flesh and a gaping wound beneath the woman's chin. Amelia's gaze lingered on the gash, noting the wound was deep enough to reveal the white of Rose's spine.

"Other than her throat, she sustained a laceration near her hip." As he finished unzipping the body bag, Dunlap didn't need to point out the bolt protruding from her back. "I'll remove that once I'm doing the autopsy."

If there were any lingering doubts about whether Amelia was dealing with the same killers, they were put to rest by the crossbow bolt staring back at her.

The hunters were already hunting again. Yet they hadn't managed to leave their signature mark on Rose Seller. Between that and failing to kill one of their targets, their stressors were racking up. Surely, now, they'd make a big enough mistake to get themselves caught sooner rather than later.

29

Amelia and Dean started work as soon as they returned to Chicago later that morning.

Mondays normally sucked, but this one was especially awful.

To Amelia's surprise, despite spending most of her time at the FBI office and having her sleep cut short, she was wide awake. Her determination to find justice for Rose Seller and ensure Sophie Hendrix's safety was more efficient fuel than any coffee on the planet.

Amelia and Dean worried about Sophie Hendrix's location, so they'd secured a transfer for the girl to an FBI safe house in Chicago where a U.S. marshal would guard her. Once her parents returned from their weekend vacation—their flight had been delayed twice so far—they would reunite with their daughter. In the meantime, the best course of action was to keep Sophie out of the public eye.

Though Amelia and Dean threw everything into following up on Rose Seller's murder, their attempts to dredge up witnesses from the campground turned up nothing. Neither Rose nor her niece had any obvious connection to the previous victims, and Layton Redker hadn't picked out another common thread between them and the thirty-nine people already killed. Their occupations and life experiences differed too greatly.

With nothing to tie the victims together, Amelia sought any pattern they hadn't explored yet.

So far, she and Dean hadn't pinned down anything peculiar about the locations either. Some were owned by the government while some were owned by private citizens or businesses. For each privately owned piece of land, they'd reached out to the owner for a quick chat, but the phone calls had resulted in nothing productive.

Still, the location bugged Amelia. Had they missed something during their first pass? *The killers must have a reason for choosing the specific places they did.*

Picking at the label on her bottled water, Amelia scanned the Northern Cardinal Campground website. The page was basic but functional. In a word, professional. Campers could register for a spot online, view a satellite map of the area, and read about the place's history. In addition, it listed the types of plant and animal life visitors could expect to encounter.

Nothing special.

As the door to the incident room swung open, Amelia held back a sigh and swiveled in her chair to greet Dean. "Welcome back. Any luck with forensics?"

Nudging the door closed, Dean heaved Amelia's sigh for her. "Yes and no. It's not really anything we didn't suspect, but the crossbow bolt found on Rose Seller's body is virtually identical to the bolt we recovered from Lake Henrietta. One of the techs is researching the bolt itself to see if there's anything distinctive about it. Maybe the killer customizes them. It may not amount to anything, but I thanked them for chasing that down for us."

"Yeah, maybe that'll help narrow our suspect pool from infinity to...fewer."

"Ha. You never know. Also, the lab confirmed that some of the blood found at the site of the struggle didn't belong to Rose or Sophie. All the foreign samples are AB positive, and Sophie and her aunt both have O negative."

Well, confirmation was better than nothing. "Sophie thinks Rose wounded both of them, but she didn't see where the woman was hit."

He held up a finger as he took his seat. "The lab'll have a more complete DNA profile soon since it's being rushed, but for now, they did say that one of the AB blood samples was from a female and the other was from a male."

"Siblings, like Sophie said. She'd heard the woman mention a brother, so it's good to get that corroborated with the DNA. Blood type is influenced by genetics, so it makes sense they both have the same blood type."

Amelia and the others had suspected the pair of killers shared a close bond. Learning they were siblings didn't surprise her, even though female serial killers were less common than their male counterparts.

The chair creaked as Dean leaned back. "And that aligns with the footprints out at Lake Henrietta. One print was definitely too small and the impression too shallow to have been created by a large person. The lab didn't find any prints on this crossbow bolt, unfortunately. But if you ask me, the blood is just as good, even if it doesn't match anyone in the system."

He was right. They'd amassed a respectable collection of evidence. They just needed to locate a suspect for comparison.

Which brought Amelia back to the other locations of the attacks. She straightened in her chair and turned back to her laptop. "Well, there's still no pattern between the victims."

"Two people each time, but that's where the similarities end." Even though they'd gone over the details ad nauseum by now, Dean began listing off what they knew, raising a finger with each point. "None of the vics were elderly, and ages ranged from seventeen to forty-six. Sixteen to forty-six if you include Sophie. Which is quite a gap, but if you think about it, they're all in the age range of 'healthy adult,' for the most part."

That reminded Amelia yet again of Layton's assessment of the killers acting like hunters. "Because they're hunting them. Hunters don't typically go after sickly prey or the extremely young or old."

"Predators do. They don't hunt for the challenge, they hunt for survival." His lips thinned. "No sport in that to humans, I guess."

"Then that could be why they pick people in this age range. None of the vics were disabled either. All healthy."

"But it's also the age range of people who go camping. And they need this type of environment to hunt."

"Meaning we can't actually determine whether they choose their targets for the location or for their health." Amelia tapped one fingertip against the side of her laptop casing. "Does the location lead them to find healthy, challenging 'prey,' or are healthy, challenging targets just more concentrated in the isolated areas they prefer?"

Chicken or egg?

During her review of the ownership records for the various campgrounds-turned-murder-sites, Amelia hadn't found anything tying the owners to the victims. She'd cross-referenced each name with the list of owners from the other scenes, but none was a match. When their speculation fell silent, she began digging into the property records for Northern Cardinal Campground.

Later, as she glanced up from her computer to reach for her water, she noted Dean's puzzled expression. "What? Did you find something?"

He blinked a few times and met her gaze. "I don't know. Probably not, but it's still interesting. Apparently, twenty-five plus years ago, Northern Cardinal Summer Camp hosted a getaway for more than a hundred kids from all over the state."

"Huh. That wasn't on their website. They must've discontinued it during one of the ownership changes. The most recent sale of the campground happened about ten years ago."

"The summer camp was really all that kept the place profitable. It made money, but it was also a big liability. Anyway." He rolled his head, grimacing as his muscles stretched. "Real estate isn't my forte. Besides, that's not what I found. Twenty-five years ago, back when the place was still a summer camp, a kid supposedly fell down a steep incline, hit his head on a rock, and wound up on life support. The family decided to take him off life support after about five years."

"Wow." Though Amelia's heart went out to the kid and his loved ones, she suspected Dean had found more than just the sad story.

"But." He dug his fingers into his neck muscle. "The incident wasn't quite that clean-cut. At least, not according to the police reports. The news reported James McKinney's death as a tragic accident, but the police report included statements from James's sister saying he was pushed."

That grabbed Amelia's full attention. "Any criminal investigation?"

"Yes and no. There are official case notes from the sheriff's department stating they suspected there might've been foul play, but in the same breath, they also noted it was one kid's word against another's. Laura McKinney accused another girl at the camp, Darla Shepard, of pushing James. Darla claimed James and Laura had bullied her and her twin brother the previous summer, and that Laura was using James's accident to frame them and get them in trouble. Which, to be honest, isn't that far-fetched. Kids that age can be cruel as hell."

Having grown up dirt-poor, Amelia knew all too well how true Dean's statement was. A bizarre point came in human development where it seemed a person discovered cruelty long before understanding and empathy. "What did the McKinney family do? Try to press charges?"

Dean's mouth hardened into a straight line. "Not criminal charges. They couldn't do that without evidence, and the Kankakee Sheriff's Department didn't have enough to charge anyone for the crime. So instead, the McKinney family tried to sue the parents of the girl Laura claimed pushed James."

Though that move struck Amelia as odd for a beat, the more she considered it, the more she sympathized with the McKinney family. If the McKinneys truly believed their son had been attacked, then it made sense they would try to do anything in their power to gain some semblance of justice. "How did that pan out?"

"Not well for the McKinneys. The girl accused of pushing James down into the creek bed, Darla Shepard, was the daughter of Constance and Randall Shepard, owner of Shepard Technologies based right here in Chicago."

Amelia didn't dabble in investing, but the name sounded familiar. Tech business was typically found in Silicon Valley and, increasingly, Austin, Texas, but the Shepards stood out as an anomaly based in the Midwest.

However, the Shepard name was more immediately familiar to Amelia.

A jolt of anticipation shot through her, and she turned back to her laptop. "Darla Shepard? Wait, she and her twin brother are co-owners of Northern Cardinal Campground." Maybe the discovery held no relevance to their case, but Amelia would sure as hell find out for sure.

"Really?" Dean wrinkled his nose. "Why would you buy a place like that after being accused of murder there as a kid?"

"Plus, they shut down the summer camp. Aside from the small fee to reserve a camping spot, the place doesn't bring in any revenue." Amelia gestured at the website pulled up on her laptop. "I mean, this is completely bare bones. It looks like it was designed by a web developer on a budget of about five bucks."

Dean snorted out a laugh. "Who knows, though? Rich people buy weird shit all the time. Maybe Darla and Garrett planned to develop it someday. Or they were still salty about being accused of murder. Or maybe they just hated summer camp so much, they decided to buy the place and shut down the camp so no one else ever had to endure it."

A twinge of humor underscored Dean's tone, letting Amelia know his theory wasn't completely serious. However, his semi-sarcastic rundown held some truth—the über-wealthy did tend to make purchases others couldn't see the wisdom in.

He held up a hand. "As luck would have it, Darla and Garrett both live in Chicago. We've talked to all the other property owners via phone so far, but since the Shepards are close, I think we could spare an hour or two to pay them a visit. I haven't heard anything from Redker or Mason yet."

Gerry Mason was a tenured FBI agent who'd accompanied Layton to the scene. They'd been sent to conduct interviews in Kankakee County.

"All right, let's do it."

Amelia suspected the Shepard twins were a long shot. After all, with the sheer number of parks and campgrounds she and Dean had investigated so far, they were bound to run into one with a dark history.

On the off chance that Darla and Garrett Shepard were a viable lead, though—or if they had information that could point Amelia and Dean toward a viable lead—then they had to take the opportunity to follow up with something in their own backyard.

Either through the investigation at Kankakee General Hospital or the upcoming interview with the Shepard twins, Amelia suspected they were getting closer.

And the closer investigators got to a serial killer, the more unpredictable that killer became.

30

As Amelia neared the covered front porch of the sprawling two-story mansion, she shot a knowing glance at Dean walking beside her.

Meeting her gaze, he responded with a barely perceptible eyebrow raise, conveying in no uncertain terms that they were on the same page.

Amelia's research on the trip to Darla Shepard's residence had yielded no criminal record for the twins, but their backgrounds were...interesting. Aside from a citation for driving under the influence more than ten years ago, Garrett Shepard's record was spotless, as was his sister's. However, the officer who'd pulled Garrett over had wound up calling for backup as Garrett had become increasingly belligerent, even going so far as threatening violence.

Why had the incident become no more than a footnote in an old misdemeanor? The answer was simple. Money. The Shepard family kept some of the best lawyers in the city on retainer, and they'd made Garrett's borderline violent outburst at a city cop disappear.

Somehow, Amelia doubted it was the first time the

Shepard family's money had covered Garrett's tracks. Likely, a person who could so easily escalate to violence had more hidden in their background than met the eye. Especially when that person's family was worth close to a billion dollars.

Memories of Stan Young and Brian Kolthoff—two exorbitantly wealthy and powerful men who'd lived out their twisted fantasies for decades before Amelia and the Bureau had taken them down—drifted to the surface of Amelia's thoughts, and she clenched her jaw to keep from grimacing.

The Shepard family was wealthy and powerful, but she mentally crossed her fingers that they weren't as well-connected and entrenched in the city's politics as Young and Kolthoff had been.

You don't even know if these two are involved with all those murders. They could be terrible people and not be murderers. Or Garrett Shepard could've been going through a rough point in his life and acted out because the stress and the booze had gotten to him.

It was true—she didn't know. All she had to base her judgment on was what she'd narrated to Dean on the drive.

Well, that and the news that the Shepard matriarch had passed only a few days earlier. The obituary Amelia found indicated Constance Shepard had passed away the previous Friday. She'd "spent her final days being comforted by her devoted daughter Darla and granddaughter Karina."

That definitely qualified as a stressor and might explain the escalation in killing. These people, if they were the killers, sure did fit the bill. Their wealth would certainly afford them the ability to hopscotch around the country. *Heck, they even own one of the campgrounds and parks.* She'd presume their innocence, but she wasn't going to bury her head in the sand.

A breeze whispered through the tall trees of the ritzy neighborhood, carrying with it the faint scent of rain. Though the sun still shined bright in the afternoon sky, a handful of thin gray clouds had begun to blot out the daylight.

Nearing a wide staircase, Amelia squared her shoulders and pressed the doorbell. Other than a muffled chime, silence greeted her. Was Darla Shepard even home? The three-car garage attached to the house was closed, leaving Amelia with no real way of knowing if the woman was here.

She looked around. The place was like an enchanted cottage meeting Windsor Palace.

As she was about to press the doorbell again, the giant door creaked inward to reveal a short woman with ebony hair tied back in a neat bun. Unless Darla Shepard's driver's license was horribly outdated or she'd miraculously shrunk six inches, gained a tan, and changed her hair color from chestnut brown, Amelia figured the woman in front of her was a housekeeper.

With a pleasant smile to the clearly puzzled woman, Amelia retrieved her badge and flipped it open. "Hello. I'm Special Agent Storm with the Federal Bureau of Investigation, and this is my partner, Special Agent Dean Steelman. We're here to speak with Darla Shepard. Is she available?"

At the words *Federal Bureau of Investigation*, the woman's posture tensed. "FBI? Of course, let me get her. Could you please wait there?"

Though the housekeeper's hesitancy to let her and Dean inside was curious, Amelia kept her expression unreadable. It also wasn't the first time she'd been made to wait on a porch or stoop. "Sure. Thank you."

Offering a nervous smile, the woman eased the door

closed, blocking Amelia and Dean from an interior view of the house.

Amelia took a step back and examined the covered porch. Towering potted ferns adorned either side of the door, coupled with twelve-foot-long cushioned stone benches. On the main floor, a large bay window extended from the facade to her left. Above, one of the second-story windows had a Juliet balcony. The stonework and brick details spoke of a family that had set down roots and had no plans to leave.

As Amelia glanced at the light mounted above the door, she spotted the dark, rounded lens of a security camera. For the most part, the camera was hidden in the metal fixture, but the placement wasn't difficult to spot for a trained observer. Nudging Dean's arm, Amelia tilted her chin up at the device.

"Huh, how 'bout that." Smiling widely, he gave the camera a cheery little wave.

The gesture was so reminiscent of Zane's brand of humor, Amelia bit the inside of her cheek to keep from laughing. In a line of work that so often dealt with the worst of what humanity had to offer, it was important to find humor in the little things.

By the time the door swung open again, Amelia and Dean were both cool and composed.

Amelia immediately recognized the woman before her as Darla Shepard.

Her eyes flitted from Dean to Amelia like a wary animal being backed into a corner. Even as the motion struck Amelia as odd, her expression cleared.

Pulling the door the rest of the way open, Darla Shepard greeted them with a welcoming, albeit slightly reserved, smile. Dressed in leggings and a loose-fitting gray t-shirt, she looked more casual than Amelia had anticipated, though the quality of the fabric suggested it probably cost more than Amelia's best suit.

Out of habit, Amelia scanned for concealed weapons or potential threats. She briefly noted a slight unevenness beneath the shirt on Darla's left shoulder but found nothing else amiss, allowing her focus to return to their impending conversation.

"Good afternoon. Veronica tells me you wanted to speak with me. How may I help you?"

Returning Darla's wooden smile, Amelia produced her badge and repeated her and Dean's introduction. "Last night, there was an...incident on a campground you and your brother own. We'd like to ask you a few questions about the property. Can we come in?"

For a split-second, Darla's expression tightened as if Amelia had just asked her for a kidney. Like her wariness from moments ago, the look vanished, replaced by another insincere smile. "Of course. Come on in."

The hairs on the back of Amelia's neck prickled as she stepped inside, but she kept her expression amiable. She couldn't put her finger on what it was about Darla Shepard that was so...off, but Amelia's instincts were screaming at her.

Was it the security camera? No, that's perfectly normal, especially for rich people. What about her being so uncomfortable when she opened the door? Sure, she's reserved, but it's not every day someone gets a visit from the Feds.

If Amelia suspected every person who tensed up at the presence of an FBI agent, she'd find herself stuck in a world of paranoia.

Logically, Darla Shepard's demeanor so far wasn't unusual. Except she hadn't expressed any concern or asked what "incident" happened at a campground she owned.

Most people would.

For the time being, Amelia would trust her instincts —*hunches*—as many veteran investigators liked to call them.

As Amelia and Dean followed Darla to a formal dining room, a man's voice drifted over from the adjacent kitchen. Amelia couldn't make out his words at first, but as she and Dean took a seat across from Darla, Amelia realized he was setting up an appointment of some sort.

Darla's gaze shifted toward the arched doorway, but her expression remained unreadable. "Sorry. My brother stopped over shortly before you arrived. Our mother passed a few days ago, and we've been quite busy setting up arrangements for her funeral." Though her words were appropriate, ice underscored her tone. Amelia couldn't imagine sounding so cold when speaking about the death of her own mother.

Amelia and Dean had agreed to act ignorant of the information they'd learned during their research. Someone losing their mother would normally squeeze at Amelia's heart. But not this time. The woman's undertone irked her. "I'm so sorry to hear that. Our condolences to you and your family."

Expression grave, Dean nodded. "We'll try to make this as quick as we can so you can get back to your day. But... since your brother is also an owner of Northern Cardinal Campground, it would be helpful for us to speak to him as well."

To her credit, if the suggestion fazed her, Darla didn't show it. "I'm sure he wouldn't mind." As she pulled out a chair across from them, she winced at the movement.

Time seemed to freeze as Amelia replayed Sophie

Hendrix's statement in her mind, each puzzle piece snapping into place.

During Sophie's attack, the assailant had been struck by her aunt's knife.

Darla's telling wince as she pulled out the chair.

The subtle unevenness beneath her shirt—possibly a bandage.

Gazing into Darla Shepard's eyes, a chilling certainty settled in Amelia's core. She was sitting face-to-face with pure evil.

And from the way Dean had stiffened beside her, he'd seen it too.

What proof did they currently have, though?

Maybe she could catch her in a lie. Keeping her tone as casual and agreeable as possible, Amelia gestured at Darla's shoulder. Though she struggled to force concern into her voice, she managed a simple, "You okay?"

Heaving a sigh, Darla sank into her seat. "It's stupid, honestly. My brother and I were out having a couple drinks the night before last, and we...we got mugged at knifepoint. I do a lot of self-defense training, and like an idiot, I tried to fight back. I should've just let him have my purse. It really wasn't worth it." Her expression grew forlorn as she gingerly touched her shoulder.

Either it was a true story, or Darla Shepard was a very convincing liar.

"It's all right, though. We're both safe, and that's what matters."

Though Amelia had caught the man in her peripheral vision as he entered the room, she swiveled her head just enough to keep the brother and sister in sight. "Absolutely. It's terrible that happened to you, but I'm glad you're both okay."

Garrett Shepard stood as tall as Dean's six-three, and his physique spoke of someone who took their workout routine seriously. With dark eyes like his sister's and a head full of chestnut-brown hair, the family resemblance was undeniable.

Unlike Darla, Garrett's smile appeared genuine as he took a seat beside his sister. He didn't display any outward signs that he was injured. "I'm Garrett Shepard. I overheard you saying you'd like to speak to me along with my sister."

Dean's sudden smile matched Garrett's energy. "Yes. Like we told her, we'll make this as quick as we can." He motioned toward Darla. "Your sister was telling us about the mugging. I'm sorry that happened to you. Did you get hurt yourself?"

Unconsciously glancing at his arm, Garrett shrugged. "Nothing serious, just a few bruises. We filed a police report, but we haven't heard anything from the officers yet. To be honest, I don't even think they took us seriously."

"Well, if you don't mind giving us the details, we can see about following up on it for you." Dean's Southern twang became more pronounced, a tactic Amelia recognized he used whenever he aimed to put someone at ease or play into the stereotypes often linked to a Southern accent.

Without waiting for her brother's input, Darla raised a hand. "No, really, that's okay. You're FBI agents, and I'm sure you're very busy. We don't want to burden you with something like a mugging, and, well..." She chewed on her bottom lip. "Honestly, we're just under so much stress right now. This is just adding to it. I'm sure the police will do a fine job. I'd just...really rather not rehash the details right now."

That was convenient. Amelia was tempted to press the siblings about the incident, to reassure them it was no big deal for her and Dean to look into the attack, but she held her tongue, because she had a much better idea. Something that would give her far more reliable results than an interrogation with a couple of people who might well be sociopaths.

Reaching into her handbag for a manila folder, Amelia offered the twins an understanding smile. "We won't pester you about it today, but we can leave you our cards so you can reach out to us if you'd like."

Darla's shoulders relaxed. "That would be perfect. Thank you."

Dean glanced at Amelia's eight-by-ten folder, but his gaze didn't linger. She hadn't cleared her strategy with him, but she'd come to realize Dean Steelman was a master at improvisation.

"All right, then. Y'all own Northern Cardinal Campground, and you've owned it for more than a decade. You mind if I ask why? Looks like you bought it for a couple million, but I doubt it's returned even half that in revenue over the past ten years."

Garrett leaned back in his chair and held out his hands. "It was a sentimental thing. We went to camp there as kids, and when we went to check the place out again after we finished college, it wasn't very well-maintained. We had the money, so we figured we might as well buy it and fix it up a little. If nothing else, we could always resell it down the line or even develop the land and make a nice little profit off it."

There was something about the way Garrett looked at her and Dean that set Amelia's hairs on end, as if he were a vampire eyeballing his next meal or a werewolf imagining how he'd rip their hearts out at the next full moon.

But what was even more unsettling was the sense of familiarity in his tone when he spoke. Amelia knew she'd never crossed paths with this man in her life, but he acted as if she and Dean were longstanding members of the same country club.

Amelia opened her envelope. "Do you two spend much time at your campground?"

Darla fiddled with her wedding ring. "Not as much as we'd like, especially lately. Our mother was sick for a while before she passed, and my daughter and I were spending what time we could with her."

"Right, of course." Amelia hoped her sympathetic tone was convincing. "And could you tell us where you were Saturday night and Sunday early morning?"

Dean retrieved a notebook and pen from his suit jacket.

"Oh, right. Saturday night is when we were...mugged." Darla gently patted her shoulder. "We went to dinner at Montanelli's Steakhouse, and then we went for drinks at The Golden Lounge. It's a martini bar not too far from Montanelli's."

"Was it just the two of you?"

Darla shifted in her seat and seemed to rush to speak before Garrett could have the chance. "Yes. Our spouses and children don't fully understand our twin bond. Instead of flaunting it, we meet for dinner and drinks periodically and enjoy an evening where we can just be ourselves."

As Dean scrawled out notes, Amelia pulled a handful of photos from the envelope. Normally, she'd have handed the twins a tablet to show them pictures, but for her plan, she needed the physical photographs.

"Are you aware that on Saturday night, at the campground you own, a woman was murdered? Her niece was attacked, as well, but fortunately, she managed to escape the scene and call for help."

Though Darla's eyes bulged at the information, Amelia

didn't buy her display of shock. "Oh my god, that's...that's terrible. What happened? Has the person been caught?"

"Not yet. That's why we're here to visit you today." Amelia purposely left the statement cryptic, and her strategy paid off.

Both Garrett's and Darla's bodies went stiff, despite their efforts to come across as surprised or horrified.

Mentioning Rose Seller and Sophie Hendrix made them nervous.

"Here." Amelia scooted the photos of Rose halfway across the table. Since Sophie had been attacked at night, she wasn't about to give them an eight-by-ten glossy of the lone survivor. "Have a look at this. We'd like to know if you recognize her."

"Of course." Darla reached for the picture, which Amelia had printed from social media. As she held it up, her eyebrows scrunched together like she was trying to solve a trigonometry equation. "I...I'm sorry, but I don't recognize her." Darla passed the photo to her brother.

Like his sister, Garrett studied the picture before shaking his head and sliding it back across the table to Amelia. "No, sorry. I don't recognize her either."

While maintaining nonchalance to distract from the fact that she wasn't touching the photograph, Amelia posed her next question for Darla and Garrett. "Do you have any records of the folks who were camping at your campground this past weekend?"

Darla appeared contemplative for a beat before nodding. "We should, yes. We can send them to you if that would help in your investigation."

"That would be very helpful, thank you. It'll save us the hassle of getting a subpoena."

It might have been Amelia's imagination, but she

could've sworn relief was palpable as Darla smiled in response. "Absolutely. We can send that to you right away."

Amelia doubted any information provided by Darla or Garrett Shepard would prove useful, but this at least covered all her bases.

As long as at least one print on the photograph of Rose was clear, she'd get all the answers she needed from the forensic lab.

31

The second Amelia and Dean returned to the office, Amelia all but raced to the forensic lab to hand over the photo of Rose. Between the fingerprint found on the crossbow at Lake Henrietta and a couple prints found at an older scene—neither of which were a match to the bolt, leading Amelia and Dean to believe they had been left by the second perpetrator—they'd have a match if either of the Shepard twins were involved.

On her short elevator trip up to the incident room, Amelia was struck by an idea. Instead of joining Dean, she moved to an empty room next door to their war room. Nudging the door shut with her hip, she uploaded several images to her phone from the FBI database. Then she dialed the contact number she had for the witness they'd moved to protective custody.

After two rings, a shaky voice answered. "Hello?"

"Sophie, this is Special Agent Amelia Storm. How are you doing?"

"Oh, hi. Sorry about that. I don't get any incoming calls

on this phone they gave me, and I wasn't sure I should answer."

"Right. We need to keep you safe until we can put the people who attacked you and your aunt behind bars. But no one has this number outside of the FBI and the Marshal service."

"Okay. That's good. I..." There was mumbling in the background. "Sorry again. My mom's here and she wants me to tell you thank you for everything you're doing to catch the people who did this."

"Well, Sophie, that's why I'm calling."

"Did you catch them?" Sophie's hope was contagious, and Amelia didn't want to disappoint her.

"Not yet. But I think you might be able to help us. We have some persons of interest, so it'd be helpful if you could look at some photos and tell us if you recognize anyone. Do you think you could do that?"

"It was pretty dark, but I did get a few glimpses of them. Especially the man while he was fighting Aunt Rose. I can try."

"Great. The phone you're using right now is a smartphone, right?"

"Yeah. But it doesn't have any games or social media apps. It's pretty lame."

Amelia stifled her chuckle when she realized how miserable it must be for a sixteen-year-old girl who'd just witnessed the murder of her own aunt to go without those distractions for even a few hours, let alone days. "Okay, is one of the marshals there with you? They need to document your responses."

"Yeah, there's..." Muffled noises followed. "Yeah, I have a lady here with me."

"I'm going to send a series of pictures through to this

phone. Take a few minutes to look through them and then let the marshal and me know if anyone looks familiar."

"Okay. Go ahead."

Amelia tapped a few keys and sent through a batch of photos of suspects who met the general physical description of Darla Shepard.

"Agent Storm?"

"Yeah, Sophie."

Sophie's voice trembled as she spoke. "The woman in photo number two is the lady who attacked us. I'm certain of it."

Yes! That's Darla.

Amelia hid her enthusiasm from the teenager. "Are you sure?"

"I didn't think I would be, but I am. Her eyes...there's just this...look. Like she doesn't feel things, if that makes sense."

To avoid indicating whether Sophie had accurately identified the person of interest, Amelia went ahead and sent the group of photos of male suspects matching Garrett's physical appearance.

Only a moment passed before Sophie exclaimed. "Oh god. It's him. Number six. That's the man who jumped out from behind the tree and fought with Aunt Rose."

"What makes you so sure it's the same man?"

"I can't explain it really, but his eyes are the same as the lady's."

"Thanks for doing that for us. Please make sure to give any other details to the marshal. I hope looking at the photos didn't upset you."

"At least it gave me something to do." Sophie cleared her throat, and Amelia realized the girl had been crying. "Agent

Storm, will you please catch them? Not for me. For Aunt Rose."

"I'm not going to rest until the people who attacked you are stopped."

After ending the call with a few promises to keep in touch, Amelia dropped into an empty chair. She hadn't been lying when she'd made that promise to Sophie.

All the puzzle pieces raced each other to see which could complete the picture first. She ran through the various details of Layton Redker's official profile on the killers. He'd speculated the duo must share a bond to trust one another with such a significant secret, and that they either traveled often for work or were wealthy enough to afford frequent travel.

The Shepard twins matched most of Layton's criteria. Darla had admitted she and her brother shared a unique closeness not even their spouses understood. Check. The Shepard family was wealthy, and with the recent death of their mother, Garrett and Darla would likely inherit a tidy sum. Check.

And, of course, there was Darla's shoulder injury.

A mugging Amelia suspected was fabricated.

Though the fingerprint analysis was on priority, she still had a little time to kill before the results would come in. More than enough time to check on Darla and Garrett's supposed alibi for Saturday night.

Fueled with renewed purpose, Amelia made her way next door to the incident room.

As she let herself inside, Dean glanced up from his laptop. "Welcome back. Got those prints to the lab?"

Amelia nudged the door closed and unshouldered her handbag. "Sure did. It isn't the best evidence collection in the world, but the lab tech was optimistic. He said glossy photos like that hold fingerprints really well."

"Good news for a change. And," he grinned at her, "quick thinking on your part. Nicely done, partner."

Pulling out her chair, Amelia paused for a quick bow. "Thank you. I also just got off the phone with Sophie Hendrix."

"Oh?"

"I threw together some pictures and texted her a photo array."

Dean leaned forward in his chair. "Don't leave me hanging, Storm."

"She positively identified both Darla and Garrett Shepard."

"Wow. Well then, let me share my news. While you were down in the lab, I took the liberty of reaching out to Montanelli's. They were a little hesitant to give me anything at first, but I asked for the manager, and he looked up their guest list from Saturday night. Guess who was there?"

For a beat, Amelia's stomach and her hopes fell to the floor. "Wait, were they there?"

"No. Their brother was, though. Eddie Shepard was there alone. The manager said Darla and Garrett are regulars, but they definitely weren't there on Saturday."

"They lied to us."

"Sure did. I guess they didn't think we'd follow up on it. I was just about to look for the police report they say they filed." Leaning back in his chair, Dean stretched both arms above his head.

Amelia's instincts had been right. Darla and Garrett Shepard were hiding something. They'd lied about their alibi. Had injuries that matched those suffered when Rose fought back. Had wealth that allowed them to hop around the country. Blood collected at the scene indicated a familial tie between the perps. And they were positively identified by the victim.

The mountain of circumstantial evidence was almost too good to be true. But what they really needed was conclusive DNA or a fingerprint match.

Before Amelia could list any more items stacked against the Shepard twins, a knock at the door jerked her attention away from her laptop. Exchanging a puzzled glance with Dean, she swiveled in her chair. "It's unlocked."

Though she expected Layton Redker or Gerry Mason to enter, a less familiar young man peeked through the opening in the door. Amelia didn't interact with the guy much, but she'd become accustomed to seeing his face at the reception desk almost every day when she came into the office.

The young man pushed the door open a little wider. "Agents Steelman and Storm?"

Dean nodded. "That's us. What can we help you with?"

"There's a visitor here who's asked to speak to the agents working on the Lake Henrietta murders. He's down in an interview room on the first floor."

"A visitor?" Amelia echoed, making no effort to conceal her surprise. "Who is it?"

The receptionist readjusted his glasses. "We've got him logged as a visitor, and we checked his ID. His name is Eddie Shepard."

32

Amelia and Dean set aside their research into Garrett and Darla's alibi and followed the receptionist down to the first floor where Eddie Shepard awaited them.

The twins looked guiltier with each new piece of evidence they uncovered. What could Eddie add that might help or hinder their case?

When Dean swung open the door, allowing Amelia to walk through first, Eddie Shepard's head snapped up from the scenic view of his folded hands. His expression held a mixture of anxiety, fear, and resolve, as if he were in the midst of a mental upheaval.

After Amelia and Dean produced their badges and ran through the usual introductions, Amelia took a seat across from Eddie as she flipped to a blank page in her notebook and clicked her pen. "We understand you'd like to speak to the investigators in charge of the Lake Henrietta murders. Could you tell us why?"

Eddie leaned forward, his gaze shifting back and forth between Dean and Amelia. "Because I think I might have some information that can help you. I think my brother and sister were involved."

Amelia fought to keep her surprise concealed. She'd expected Eddie to have something to say about his siblings, but she hadn't anticipated his candor. "And do you have anything to support this accusation, Mr. Shepard?"

Blowing out a long breath, Eddie straightened his back. "The news said one of the victims was killed with a crossbow."

Propping his elbows on the table, Dean clasped his hands in front of his chest. "That's right."

"Well, my sister, Darla, has had a fascination with crossbows since she was in high school. She's got an entire indoor archery range that she doesn't let anyone else into. Well, no one aside from Garrett anyway. Those two have always been as thick as thieves, ever since they were born."

The Shepard twin bingo card of guilt was quickly filling up.

"Have you gone inside your sister's range?"

"No. She's very protective of it. I don't know a lot about archery, but the crossbow isn't so much used in recreational archery as it is in hunting. Darla isn't entering archery competitions, and I guarantee you she's not a fan of the outdoors." Eddie's hands had curled into fists on the table. "The news said the woman who was killed at the park my siblings own had her throat slit. And that the girl who survived was shot with a crossbow."

That was certainly interesting information. Adding it to the rest of the pile further damned Eddie's brother and sister. Tempering her excitement, Amelia decided to keep the details of their case close to the vest, just in case. "Okay. Do you have anything else?"

Eddie flexed his hands, his jaw tightening. "There's

plenty. Does the name James McKinney mean anything to you?"

Hell, yeah, it does.

Dean pulled out his phone and went through the process of asking for permission to record the conversation before answering Eddie's question. "James McKinney fell down a steep decline and hit his head on a rock. Authorities ruled his eventual death years later an accident."

A scowl darkened Eddie's face. "That wasn't an accident. Darla pushed that kid down into the creek one summer at camp. I knew it, my parents knew it, but they still spent a small fortune to keep it under wraps. To save face. They couldn't court politicians and buy influence if their daughter was accused of murdering some kid at summer camp."

Eddie's tone was about as joyful as a funeral director's, but it held no anxiety or other indication of a lie. Granted, the so-called "science of reading body language" was far from scientific, but Amelia's time at the Bureau had given her a good sense for suspicious behavior. Certain body language cues were only one factor she used.

Plus, the disdain with which Eddie referred to his younger siblings was as obvious as the daylight outside. His willingness to come speak against his siblings piqued her interest.

Before Amelia or Dean could pose a follow-up question, Eddie patted the table. "All right, you're probably questioning my sincerity, and I don't blame you. It's a long story, but I'll try to sum it up. Darla and Garrett are...wrong."

He fell quiet for so long that Amelia took it upon herself to prompt him. "Wrong?"

Eddie tapped his temple. "Something in their heads is broken, and it's been like that since they were little kids.

When they were six, they'd hit and cut each other and then tell our parents that I was the one who'd done it. Mom and Dad believed them the first few times, but then they started to catch on to the pattern."

Amelia's heart squeezed for the man in front of her. It was obvious he wasn't just hurting now but had been hurting for many years.

"I couldn't even tell you why my brother and sister did it." Eddie threw up his hands. "Just for something to do, I think. If you ask me, my parents both knew there was something wrong with Darla and Garrett. They didn't want it to be true, but deep down, they knew."

He was leading up to something terrible. Amelia could tell from the look on his face.

Leaning back in his chair, Eddie heaved a weary sigh. "When I was sixteen and they were ten, they put antifreeze in my drink, and I wound up in the ER. You know how we tell college girls to never leave their drink unattended when they're at a party? Yeah, that was me until I moved out. To this day, I'll dump out my drink if I accidentally leave it unattended."

Licking her lips, Amelia chose her next words carefully. She had no reason to doubt Eddie and had a growing list of reasons to suspect the Shepard twins—but as an investigator, she needed corroboration.

She met Eddie's gaze. "I'm sorry you had to experience that, Mr. Shepard. And I hate to sound insensitive, but is any of this documented?"

Eddie chuckled dryly. "I knew you'd ask that. Yes. My mother kept a journal until the day she died, and she wrote about it in there. There're also the hospital records to back it up. My mother is dead now, but I'm in charge of her possessions, so neither Darla nor Garrett have had a chance to destroy anything."

From there, Eddie detailed his younger siblings' warped development. Everything in his recollection was in line with the signs psychologists searched for in budding sociopaths and serial killers, and if Layton Redker had been present, he'd have marveled at the consistency.

Where Eddie received the attention of a caring nanny during the critical years of his development, Garrett and Darla hadn't shared in his fortune. Their parents had treated them more as accessories than human beings, and the twins were subjected to a constantly changing stream of housekeepers and nannies.

Between the neglect and their parents' negative attitudes toward their children, Garrett and Darla turned to other avenues to receive the attention they desired. Namely, by tormenting their older brother. When that stopped working, they eventually moved on to classmates. Both twins were ultimately kicked out of their ritzy private school for violent acts against other students, and they finished their high school diplomas in a public school district.

Amelia was no psychologist, but she figured there was a possibility Darla and Garrett could have turned their lives around as they reached adulthood. A fair amount of brain growth and development occurred from ages seventeen to the mid-twenties, and plenty of "troubled" children went on to lead regular, healthy lives.

The main differentiating factor was whether they received help.

As Eddie finished explaining how his mother had cut Darla and Garrett out of her will, Amelia's phone buzzed once in her pocket. If she hadn't been waiting for a crucial message from forensics, she'd have ignored the notification.

Holding up a hand and offering an apology, she retrieved her phone to check the sender. Just as she'd hoped, the notification was for an email from forensics. Barely tempering her excitement, she pushed to her feet. "Just a second. This is important."

Shoving the door open, Amelia stepped into the hall and opened the email. She scrolled past the details of certain ridges, test specifics, and other information to get to the results. When she reached the synopsis, her breath caught in her throat as her entire body tensed in anticipation.

Both unique prints from the photograph—one from Darla, and one from Garrett—were a match to the two unique prints from the crime scenes.

Bingo!

33

Dragging my suitcase into the garage, I swallowed a series of four-letter words as I spotted my daughter sitting on a bench next to the doorway. As soon as the two FBI agents had departed earlier that afternoon, my brother and I had scrambled to prepare ourselves for an international vacation. At first, we'd considered leaving with just the two of us, but we'd quickly revised that plan.

The FBI sniffing around my house was a bad sign, but at the same time, I could use it as an opportunity. We needed to get the hell out of the United States, and our plan was to drive out to the private airport that housed Garrett's Cessna. From there, we'd fly to Cuba. The plane easily had the range, and unlike Mexico and many other Latin American countries, Cuba had no extradition agreement with the U.S.

Once we were there, we could work out the specifics of where to go next. For now, the mission was to get as far away as possible.

The kids were also the keys to our family's money. If we left them, then our good-for-nothing spawn and worthless spouses would inherit a fortune and we'd be left paupers.

Provided we could even access the measly sum we'd been left.

We could also imprison the children if necessary. Then, when they turned eighteen, they could have their freedom.

For a price.

They could turn over their trusts to us or remain in Cuba in a custom-made hell just for them. The choice would be theirs.

I silently reminded myself of the plan as I tossed my suitcase into the trunk of my Mercedes. "What are you doing?"

My daughter's head snapped up from her paperback. I'd already confiscated her phone so she couldn't send an SOS to Eddie or her father.

I mentally patted myself on the back for how I'd distracted my husband. He had no idea the work email sending him on an errand to Dekalb was from me. He'd always been fiercely loyal to my family's business, and I'd known damn well he wouldn't question a message asking him to meet with a prospective client out of town. Garrett, on the other hand, had merely ordered his wife to go grocery shopping.

Sometimes, I envied his ability to control that woman. My husband wasn't half as obedient as Imelda, but then again, there was a reason my brother had picked a woman more than ten years his junior.

I turned my attention back to my daughter, disgusted. "What the hell are you doing? Have you even packed anything yet?"

She shifted in her seat, clearly uncomfortable. "You didn't say where we're going. Where's Dad? Why can't I just stay home with him? It's a school night, and I have home—"

"I didn't ask for excuses! Either go get your shit right now, or you'll be leaving without it!"

The girl shrank back, and my disgust for her grew.

"B-but..."

"No!" I took a menacing step toward her and raised my hand. Anger flared in my veins like acid, and if this little brat didn't cooperate soon, she wouldn't live to see her eighteenth birthday.

Her book fell to the floor as she snapped both arms up defensively.

"You know what? You don't get to bring anything. Get in the fucking car, and don't make me tell you again."

Eyes glassy, hands trembling, the girl swallowed, but she didn't protest.

For emphasis, I jabbed a finger in the direction of the sedan. "Car. *Now*."

As my daughter moved on unsteady feet, I permitted myself a moment of victory in a day otherwise marked by chaos and upheaval.

My brother and I would be fine. If I could control this little brat so we could get out of the country, we'd be home free. We'd find a hideout, hunker down, and figure a way out of this.

34

Warrant in hand, Dean pounded his fist on the front door of Garrett Shepard's home. The fingerprint evidence had been enough to secure warrants for both Shepard twins' properties, and he and Amelia had decided to divide and conquer.

"FBI. We have a warrant. Open up."

Under normal circumstances, Dean would have given the occupants at least a few minutes to answer. These circumstances weren't normal. Not with thirty-nine people dead.

He stepped back and nodded to the SWAT leader. A second later, the door burst open and the team swarmed in. Dean followed, weapon up and ready. He was disappointed as calls of, "Clear," echoed throughout the home.

Shit. The place was empty.

His sense of urgency intensified.

Dean pulled out his phone to call Amelia, silently praying that she'd had better luck.

"Wh-what's happening?"

Dean turned to find a woman standing in the front door

of the home. Her wavy shoulder-length hair was just as neatly styled as it was in her driver's license photo, and her cream-colored blouse, leggings, and flats gave the air of a well-off woman. Her terrified expression was proof to her identity.

Imelda Shepard.

Dean retrieved his badge and flipped it open. "I'm Special Agent Dean Steelman. You must be Imelda Shepard. Is that right?"

Imelda swiped at her nose with the back of one trembling hand. "Y-yes...that's me. What's going on here? Who are all these people? Why is the FBI in my house? Wh-what's happening here?" The volume of her voice grew with each frantic question.

Though Dean didn't figure Imelda was involved in Garrett's twisted extracurricular activities, he wasn't foolish enough to write off the possibility entirely.

He reached into his suit jacket for a copy of the signed warrant. "We have a warrant to search the house. Your husband wasn't home when we got here. Do you know where he is?"

Sniffling, Imelda shook her head. "No. He was home when I left. He asked me...told me to go to the store to get food for dinner. Please tell me my kids are here."

A stone sank in Dean's stomach. "There's no one here."

Tears sprang to Imelda's eyes as she covered her mouth with a hand. "Oh no, no, no, no, no. My babies. Where are my babies? Did he take them? Where did he take them? Where are they? Please, you have to help me find them."

Dean had a million questions, but at the same time, he suspected he knew the answer to most of them. For the past decade, Imelda had lived under a roof with a murderous sociopath. Not just any murderous sociopath, but a wealthy, powerful man with whom she had two young children.

Imelda Shepard wasn't an accomplice. She was another victim.

Coupled with Eddie's recollection of Constance Shepard's will, Dean could fill in the blanks. Garrett Shepard was one of the prime suspects in thirty-nine homicides, and he'd now kidnapped his two children.

"Okay, Imelda. I can help you, but I need you to help me, too, all right?"

Without hesitating, she nodded. "Of course. Whatever you need."

"Do you know where your husband would go if he was trying to…get away from the city? Far away?" Dean didn't want the poor woman to panic, but at the same time, he had to make the urgency of the situation clear.

"Yes, he'd go to his plane. He keeps it in the hangar at DuPage."

From his and Amelia's research on the Shepard twins, Dean knew exactly the plane she was referencing. A Cessna Longitude, capable of flying thousands of miles before stopping to refuel. If Garrett got to that damn plane, he'd be as good as gone, and so would the children he'd taken.

"That's helpful." Dean caught the eye of an officer hovering a few feet away at her station near the door. "Will you sit with Mrs. Shepard while I make a call?"

With a knowing look, the officer escorted the distraught woman to her police car. Even though Dean believed Imelda innocent, he wouldn't take any chances.

Pulling up Amelia's number on his phone, he barely gave her time to answer before nearly shouting. "Anything at Darla's?"

"Empty." Amelia sounded as grim as he felt. "Looks like

they knew we were coming. Officer outside didn't see anything, so we don't know which way they went. Did you find anything?"

"No, and it's the same here. But Imelda Shepard, Garrett's wife, just arrived. She's terrified and says she doesn't know where Garrett and the kids are."

Amelia cursed under her breath. "Okay, we need to act fast. Let's put out a BOLO on both Shepard siblings. We need descriptions of the kids for Amber alerts."

"Already on it." Dean waved another officer over and asked him to get pictures of the Shepard kids from Imelda. As close as the siblings were, he bet Imelda would have pictures of Darla's daughter too.

"Yes, sir." The young officer took off at a run.

Dean put his phone on speaker and opened up his messaging app. "Garrett has a Cessna Longitude housed at DuPage."

"We need to check if he filed a flight plan." Though not every private flight would require one, she was right. "I'll call the airport. I'll also send officers ahead and alert airport security."

"Good." His thumbs flew over his keyboard as he typed out instructions. "I'm also getting Agent Gerry Mason to pull the GPS from the Garretts' cars."

"Hold on." She spoke to someone, her hand half muffling the conversation. She was back a few seconds later. "Cell phone triangulation. We need to locate their phones if they're still on." Dean could almost picture Amelia's determined face. "We should also keep an eye on any financial activity...ATM withdrawals, credit card usage. Anything that can help us track them."

The moment Dean finished typing his instructions, he strode toward the door. There were about a thousand other things they'd have to do, but he could make those calls on the way. First, he needed to get to the airport. "I'm heading to DuPage."

"It's a half an hour away." The sound of her feet slapping on concrete told him everything he needed to know. Amelia was heading there too. "Meet me at the chopper."

35

Amelia, Dean, and Layton Redker were out of the Bureau helicopter as soon as it touched the ground. Less than an hour west of Chicago, the DuPage private airport catered to private businesses and individuals, and also served as a more private location for traveling celebrities and politicians. A glittering glass building sprawled out before them, behind which was a collection of hangars, runways, and a massive tarmac. It wasn't the size of Midway, but DuPage was still a significant airport.

For Garrett and Darla Shepard, it was just the right size to make an escape from the United States.

Admittedly, part of Amelia hoped the twins had been stupid enough to try driving to a different city. It'd be easier to intercept them in a car than it would be to stop them from taking off in a damn plane.

And she really didn't want to contact the military if they did manage to take off without authorization. Ever since the 9/11 terrorist attacks on New York City, airports had become some of the most heavily monitored locations in the country.

In the unlikely event a pilot managed to take off in a stolen aircraft, the military took matters into its own hands. Even with three innocent children on board, they wouldn't think twice about scrambling fighter jets when they learned the pilot of the rogue plane was the prime suspect in thirty-nine murders. And if the aircraft posed a threat to the public...

Amelia didn't want to think about that.

Chest heaving, calf muscles burning, Amelia slowed to a stop at the edge of the small lounge area before the entrance to hangar seven. Plenty of hangars for larger planes were detached from the building, but they were fortunate that the Shepard family had spent extra to have their plane located in a spot they could reach through a walkway connected to the airport itself.

Though DuPage was only about half the size of O'Hare, the jaunt had taken far more time than Amelia would've preferred.

Air traffic control grounded all outgoing flights. Garrett and Darla won't receive permission to take off.

Despite the mental reassurance, a pit remained in her stomach.

The Shepard twins had made their disdain for human life evident in their ten-year killing spree. Both twins were narcissistic to a severe degree, and Amelia suspected they wouldn't let the orders of air traffic control stop their grand escape. Even if they knew they'd be shot down by fighter jets, would they care?

Admittedly, if it was just the two of them, Amelia's worry would be markedly lower. Being blown to pieces by a fighter jet was a fitting end for them, even though Amelia would rather see the twins rot away in a jail cell for the rest of their lives.

Their kids were a different story. None of their children had chosen to have monstrous parents, nor had they consented to this impromptu flight to God only knew where. If Garrett got the Cessna off the ground and the Air Force had to intercept the plane…

Amelia wouldn't let it come to that, no matter what.

Pulling in a much-needed breath, she retrieved her service weapon as she and Dean hurried past the lounge to the double doors. Amelia took the left side, and he took the right, allowing the SWAT team to take their place.

Airport security had already alerted them to the fact that the door was locked and barricaded.

Dean held up a hand. "All right, on three." He lifted three fingers and started the countdown.

As he closed his fist, Amelia winced at the sound of metal colliding with metal. It took SWAT three tries to get through the door, but she was right on their heels the moment it flew open.

She had no idea what to expect when they emerged in the sterile white space. Part of her mind—the portion still stuck overseas in the Middle East—insisted she was about to barrel into a firefight, while the more pessimistic part of her worried the Cessna would already be gone.

As Amelia stepped onto the polished white floor, the roar of the Cessna's engine greeted her. It was like a brick wall to the face, but she couldn't waste even a second dwelling on how ungodly loud the air had become.

Her gaze shot straight toward the hangar door across the way.

It was almost three quarters of the way open, the mechanical whine barely discernable over the noise of the plane.

Shit, shit, shit! They're going to try to take off after all.

She had to remind herself that airport security was on the other side, but still...

Glaring down the sights of her Glock, she scanned the immediate area to ensure neither Garrett nor Darla were lying in wait. Aside from a couple shelves of equipment and a handful of small vehicles—a golf cart, an aircraft tug tow, and a mobile maintenance platform—the enormous hangar was empty.

With the control for the hangar door across the room, Amelia's options were limited. Her assumption that Garrett and Darla would choose to ignore the commands of air traffic control was correct, and she was in the midst of witnessing the consequences of the twins' reckless actions.

They had to know they wouldn't get far.

But her options? They were dwindling with every passing second.

She could take off across the hangar as fast as possible in hopes she'd reach the hangar door before Garrett could steer the plane onto the tarmac, but would he be able to drive his monster of a plane right through it? She wasn't sure. Planes moved slowly at the start, but the Cessna was already nudging toward the opening.

Firing her weapon would be useless. Though the Cessna wasn't as durable as a military aircraft, it was still meant to withstand some of the most extreme conditions on the planet. A 9mm handgun would be like using a slingshot to take down an eighteen-wheeler. And with ricochet risks, she'd endanger herself and others.

What did that leave her with? Sprint up to the side of the plane and flail her arms in hopes Garrett or Darla would come to their senses and stop their suicidal scheme?

Yeah, right.

A desperate plan began to form. Her eyes lingered on

the vehicles by the wall. Could she block the plane's path? But what if Garrett decided to barrel through anyway, unmindful of the potential harm to the children aboard?

She was torn. Amelia's thoughts turned to the seven, ten, and fourteen-year-old kids on board. Her snap decision would mean life or death for the three of them. They'd spent their short lives under the thumbs of their narcissistic parents, but right now, Amelia had the opportunity to provide them with a brighter future. For them to learn to drive, graduate high school, fall in love...

She had to do something, even if that meant putting her own safety in jeopardy. Granted, it wasn't a death sentence necessarily, but the timing would be tight. Amelia had to get the vehicle in front of the plane, then leap out before it hit her.

It was risky, but it was her only shot. Zane would yell at her if he were here, but he'd do the same thing if he were in her position.

Like freeing a stuck record, the world roared back to full speed.

Taking off in a sprint, Amelia headed toward the line of small vehicles and other equipment near the opening. Dean yelled her name, but she ignored him.

Choosing the tug tow, she hoped she'd made the right decision. If the squat piece of machinery was powerful enough to pull an airplane, maybe it could stop one.

As she jumped in the seat, she spotted her partner making a beeline for the golf cart. *Guess I wasn't the only one with that idea.*

It took a moment to find the ignition, and her fingers trembled only a little as she turned the key. As she wrenched the wheel to the right, she pressed down on the gas pedal. The tug zipped away from its spot against the wall only a little faster than a turtle.

Damn.

She growled in frustration as the Cessna's nose steadily advanced beyond the hangar's edge.

Not today, asshole.

Driving directly toward the plane's landing gear, she felt minuscule in the tug compared to the towering jet. She caught a fleeting glimpse of Dean's golf cart, its comical "Follow me" sign contrasting the gravity of the situation. In that instant, she felt an unexpected kinship—a bond only found in the heart of battle.

The Cessna kept advancing. Only a few feet remained before the plane collided with Amelia's vehicle. With just seconds to spare, she threw herself from the driver's seat, hitting the ground hard and rolling away. A deafening crunch echoed as metal collided with metal.

She risked a glance back. The Cessna's progress was momentarily halted, the tug crumpled beneath its weight. Relief flooded her as she watched Dean dive to safety, too, leaving the golf cart in front of a back set of wheels.

But Garrett wasn't done. The plane's engines roared louder, desperate to push past the blockade.

Amelia was pulled away as the SWAT team converged, circling the nose of the plane like predators. She clamped her hands over her ringing ears as one of the team fired a shot at the pilot's window.

The engines only roared louder.

That man was crazy.

From the corner of Amelia's eye, movement at the side of the plane caught her attention. Taking a few steps back, she realized what she'd seen.

The door had popped open.

From the darkness within, a silhouette stumbled out—a frantic teenager, clutching a younger child close to her chest and dragging another behind her. Their escape was frenzied, so desperate that their feet tangled together, sending all three tumbling to the ground in a heap.

The children were trying to save themselves from their own parents.

Gritting her teeth, Amelia sprinted toward them. Her every instinct screamed at her to protect the innocent, especially from the menace of the people who were supposed to love them the most. But as she skidded to a stop, shielding the kids from the plane's entrance, she found herself staring into the deadly aim of a crossbow.

Darla Shepard's gaze, cold and unyielding, met hers. But even as Darla's finger twitched near the trigger, Amelia's own Glock aimed squarely at her adversary's chest.

You're Amelia Storm's target now...bitch.

Time lost all meaning. The deafening drone of the engines faded into the background, replaced by the piercing intensity of the standoff. The two women were locked in a silent battle of wills, each gauging the other's intent.

"FBI! Drop your weapon! Now!"

The ball was in Darla's court. Would she relent or escalate the situation further?

Let's see how she handles a trained agent instead of a scared camper.

Behind Amelia, footsteps approached, accompanied by the sounds of readying weapons—the SWAT team closing in, muzzles trained on the aircraft and its occupants. Dean called the children to safety.

"There's no way out, Darla. Think of your daughter."

The statement was almost laughable, but for a moment, raw emotion flickered in Darla's eyes. Yet it wasn't love. Not even regret. All that was left in the woman was fear, defiance, and desperation.

Almost imperceptibly, her grip on the crossbow slackened. She glanced toward the cockpit, perhaps considering making a final, desperate move, but the odds were clearly against her.

Darla lifted her chin. "I won't go to prison."

"Prison or Hell." Amelia lifted the Glock an inch. "Your choice."

A choked sob escaped Darla's lips. With one final, resentful glare, the crossbow dropped to her feet with a dull thud. Almost immediately, two SWAT officers closed in. Two more followed, but Amelia had already turned away.

Harnessing her weapon, Amelia walked over to the children…the only ones who mattered now.

Darla and Garrett's reign of terror was over. The battle was won, but for so many families, the journey to healing had only just begun.

36

Biting into the buttery, chocolatey delight of a freshly baked chocolate croissant, Amelia let out a contented sigh. Two and a half weeks after she'd driven a tug tow in front of Garrett Shepard's Cessna Longitude, Amelia was glad to fall back into her usual work routine.

Namely, the routine of stuffing her face with chocolate croissants during her lunch break. She'd have to burn off all the extra calories when she went for her next workout, but she didn't care.

From where he sat in the booth across from her, Zane shot her a knowing grin. "You know, I wonder every morning if this is finally going to be the day when you discover the recipe for these things and retire from the FBI to become a baker." He held up his hands. "Not that it's a bad thing. If you want to open a shop that only sells chocolate croissants, more power to you."

"Oh, please." Amelia slid the little box over to him. "You love them just as much as I do."

With a grin, he snatched up the last croissant and took a

bite. "Fair point. We can both work at the bakery. What do you say we get started on it when the Shepard trial is over?"

Amelia's laugh came out more akin to a snort. "Whenever that is. Their parents' entire inheritance went to their brother and their kids, but they've still got plenty of money to waste on expensive lawyers."

Zane lifted a shoulder. "Not like it'll matter. The U.S. Attorney has DNA evidence, fingerprints, footprints, and a witness. Juries love those things. What's the defense even going to say? That someone else put Darla's and Garrett's blood at the scene where they murdered someone?"

He had a point. The prosecution's case was solid, to say the least.

That's what happens when someone leaves behind twenty different crime scenes. Not to mention the score of charges they racked up at the airport.

Darla and Garrett Shepard had fancied themselves the highest order of intelligence, but over the years, they'd become lax. As a result, the prosecutor had a veritable mountain of evidence to work with, and the defense had... well, not much.

"I'm just glad the judge denied them both bail."

"How are their kids doing, by the way? Have you and Steelman been in contact with them?"

Amelia's heart grew a little lighter as she thought of how much more hopeful Karina and her two cousins seemed after Garrett and Darla had been arrested. Karina's account of her mother's abuse was hair-raising enough on its own, but when it was coupled with Imelda's recollections of life with Garrett Shepard, it painted a terrifying picture.

"They seem like they're doing better. The Assistant U.S. Attorney is trying to build her case without having them testify, and I think she should be able to keep them out of the courtroom. Aside from testifying to their parents' character in sentencing, there isn't much they could provide to the prosecution."

"True. At least they still have one loving parent each in Winston and Imelda." Zane punctuated his observation with another giant bite of croissant. "You've got a briefing this afternoon...a new case?"

"Yep. Actually, I think I got a text about it a few minutes ago. I almost forgot." Amelia wiped her hands on a napkin and reached for her coffee. There was something pleasant about washing down a sweet treat with a nice hot latte, even toward the end of May.

When she pulled her phone from her handbag, sure enough, a blinking light told her she had a new message. She tapped in her PIN and opened the text from fellow Violent Crimes Agent Sherry Cowen.

Hey, Storm. Just got some details about our new case. Wanted to send them to you so you'll know what we'll be looking at in the briefing this afternoon.

Attached was a document, and as Amelia scanned the text, the sweet flavor on her tongue turned sour.

"What is it?" Zane's tone was equal parts concerned and curious.

"My next case. Some lunatic's been targeting social media influencers and burning their faces with acid. He's been using their accounts to post pictures of their disfigured faces after he kills them."

"Jesus Christ." Zane shook his head. "I swear, the nasty things serial killers do to their victims will never cease to amaze me."

"Yeah, me neither." Amelia pocketed her cell as her mind switched firmly into work mode.

She suspected the grotesque murders investigated by the

VCU would never become business as usual to her, and she couldn't decide whether that was a good thing or a bad thing. Only time would tell.

For now, Amelia had another deranged killer to track down.

37

Standing at the door of his lavish hotel room, Bogdan Kopeykin surveyed the space with an approving nod. The suite was a vast improvement over his apartment in Yakutsk, as was the weather outside. He'd been nervous during his flight from Russia to Chicago, but now that he'd arrived, he was immensely grateful he'd made the decision to relocate. Complete with a visa for his newest identity, Boris Ivanov, he was right at home in the new environment.

With a contented sigh, he approached the minibar to prepare himself a drink. Though vodka in America didn't quite meet his standards, he could deal with this one minor inconvenience. It wasn't like he didn't have plenty of money to import his own vodka, if it came to that.

Bogdan chuckled to himself. He could live in luxury for the rest of his days, and he'd still die a wealthy man.

But his trip to America was about much more than money.

I am here for you, Mischa Bukov. I know you are in this city somewhere, and will find you. I am going to make you pay for what you did to my brother...what you did to me.

Ever since Rurik had been brutally murdered right in front of him, Bogdan had vowed vengeance on the man responsible. At first, he'd searched for Mischa in Russia, as he'd assumed the man was a native.

But the more he'd searched, the more questions he'd unearthed. Before long, he lost his certainty Mischa Bukov even *was* Mischa Bukov.

Was the man part of the Russian KGB? The American CIA?

Upon following the arrest and prosecution of his close friend, Lou, Bogdan had learned the man was neither. He was an agent of America's FBI.

Lou Sherman's arrest and sentencing had been a setback for sure, but there was a silver lining. If it wasn't for Lou being raided and arrested by the FBI, it would've taken Bogdan years, maybe even decades, to figure out which organization Mischa Bukov belonged to.

Lifting his glass of whiskey, Bogdan sighed. "This one is for you, Lou. In seeking vengeance for my brother, so, too, will I avenge your imprisonment."

Revenge was a dish best served cold, and fortunately Bogdan was a patient man. He'd feel out the city of Chicago, maybe even find a participant for a new snuff film.

Eventually, he'd come across a clue about Mischa's identity, but getting there was half the fun.

The End
To be continued...

ACKNOWLEDGMENTS

How does one properly thank everyone involved in taking a dream and making it a reality? Here goes.

In addition to our families, whose unending support provided the foundation for us to find the time and energy to put these thoughts on paper, we want to thank the editors who polished our words and made them shine.

Many thanks to our publisher for risking taking on two newbies and giving us the confidence to become bona fide authors.

More than anyone, we want to thank you, our readers, for clicking on a couple of nobodies and sharing your most important asset, your time, with this book. We hope with all our hearts we made it worthwhile.

Much love,
Mary & Amy

ABOUT THE AUTHOR

Mary Stone lives among the majestic Blue Ridge Mountains of East Tennessee with her two dogs, four cats, a couple of energetic boys, and a very patient husband.

As a young girl, she would go to bed every night, wondering what type of creature might be lurking underneath. It wasn't until she was older that she learned that the creatures she needed to most fear were human.

Today, she creates vivid stories with courageous, strong heroines and dastardly villains. She invites you to enter her world of serial killers, FBI agents but never damsels in distress. Her female characters can handle themselves, going toe-to-toe with any male character, protagonist or antagonist.

Discover more about Mary Stone on her website.
www.authormarystone.com

Amy Wilson

Having spent her adult life in the heart of Atlanta, her upbringing near the Great Lakes always seems to slip into her writing. After several years as a vet tech, she has dreams of going back to school to be a veterinarian but it seems another dream of hers has come true first. Writing a novel.

Animals and books have always been her favorite things, in addition to her husband, who wanted her to have it all.

He's the reason she has time to write. Their two teenage boys fill the rest of her time and help her take care of the mini zoo that now fills their home with laughter...and yes, the occasional poop.

Connect with Mary Online

- facebook.com/authormarystone
- x.com/MaryStoneAuthor
- goodreads.com/AuthorMaryStone
- bookbub.com/profile/3378576590
- pinterest.com/MaryStoneAuthor
- instagram.com/marystoneauthor
- tiktok.com/@authormarystone

Printed in Great Britain
by Amazon